MW01139653

Operation Silent Moon

© 2015 Jay Argent

All Rights Reserved. No part of this publication may be reproduced, distributed, or transmitted in any form or by any means, including photocopying, recording, or other electronic or mechanical methods, without the prior written permission of the author, except in the case of brief quotations embodied in critical reviews and certain other noncommercial uses permitted by copyright law.

First Edition, 2015

ISBN-13: 978-1518776090
ISBN-10: 1518776094

Jay Argent
jay.argent@outlook.com

Operation Silent Moon

Jay Argent

Background

South Sudan gained its independence from the Republic of Sudan on July 9, 2011. Ever since, the country has suffered from a Civil War. Experts estimate that the ethnic conflicts have killed up to 100,000. Many of the 11 million citizens are on the brink of starvation, and two million people have fled their homes.

In December 2013, the Pentagon announced it was sending 150 US Marines to Africa for a mission to evacuate Americans in South Sudan. Evacuation of the US embassy staff in Juba, the capital of South Sudan, started in January 2014. Simultaneously, the consular services to US citizens were put on hold.

In May 2014, Secretary of State John Kerry travelled to the region to broker a peace deal. The cease-fire he negotiated lasted only days. Several other peace plans have failed since then, and the humanitarian disaster has only grown worse.

On August 26, 2015, South Sudan's president Salva Kiir Mayardit signed a peace deal aimed at ending the conflicts. However, in his speech to African leaders, President Kiir said that he had "serious reservations." Only time will tell what the future of the youngest nation in the world will look like.

While all above is true, this book is entirely a work of fiction. Any resemblance to real persons, events that occurred in South Sudan, or actual military operations is purely coincidental.

Chapter 1

Corporal Dennis Benson parked his navy blue Chevrolet Impala in front of his small house on Playa Del Rey Avenue, carried his grocery bags inside, and changed his Marine uniform to casual jeans and a t-shirt. He turned on the TV and browsed a couple of channels but switched it off when he saw every channel was just advertising some useless things to buy for Christmas. He hated commercials—besides, he did not have anybody he wanted to buy presents for.

The holiday season was approaching rapidly. The shop windows throughout the Camp Pendleton Marine Corps training base were full of Santas, gift boxes, and other Christmas decorations designed to lure customers. The shop owners were smiling joyfully when people sacrificed their last money to celebrate the savior's birthday. What should have been the happiest time of the year made Dennis feel annoyed and lonely.

Holding a bottle of warm beer in his hand, Dennis walked back to his bedroom and admired his figure in the mirror. Despite his boyish face, he was a 24-year-old Marine in an elite unit and sculpted muscles decorated his thin body, making him look like the male models in the porn videos he watched to jerk off every night, unless he was able to find someone to hook up with. Finding one-night company might not have been difficult with his looks, but Dennis wanted to be careful and not mix his private life with his work at Camp Pendleton. He found the guys off the base, never brought them to his home, and seldom met the same guy twice.

The bedroom was clean, almost too tidy and nicely decorated to be a single man's bedroom. Only the top drawer of the dark wooden dresser was partly open, revealing a collection of neatly folded underwear. On the dresser was a picture of Dennis together with his parents. It had been taken the same day he'd graduated from high school, and he was dressed in that funny gown and even funnier hat. His parents were smiling and looked proud, which had changed soon after. Seeing his father's face made him angry, and he took the picture and put it away in the drawer.

After noticing that he was already late, Dennis locked the door and walked to the nearby bar. All of his teammates lived in the neighborhood, and they had agreed to celebrate their graduation. Since all of them had received additional sniper training at boot camp, the military had assigned them to the Force Reconnaissance Company, which would likely mean more direct action missions compared to an ordinary Marine recon team.

The bartender greeted Dennis enthusiastically when he stepped in. He nodded and smiled to the cute guy and then scanned the gloomy room to find his buddies. Soon he noticed them at the back of the room.

"Good evening, shitheads," Dennis greeted his team and sat next to Private Brian Newton.

"The cocky boy finally arrives," Newton said and gave Dennis a friendly pat on his back.

"What do you know about his cock?" Private Ethan Mullen asked. He was sitting on the other side of the table.

"None of your business, jackass," Newton said, smiling. "But if you really want to know, I know everything about that shrimp of his."

"Ha-ha. It's bigger than yours together," Dennis said, enjoying the company of his teammates.

Sergeant Adler Williams sighed. "Guys, Benson just got here, and all you want to talk about is his drumstick," he said.

"We could also talk about boobs and pussy, but Newton and Mullen are too young for that," Dennis said, even though the topic could not have interested him less.

This was their four-member recon team. Sergeant Williams, who was two years older than Dennis, was the team leader. Having spent the last year together at the training camp, Dennis considered these three men his closest friends and would trust his life in their hands at any time without a single doubt. That was what it meant to be a Marine for him.

Williams ordered them a new round of beers, and Newton took a worn-out deck of cards from his pocket. Everybody recognized the deck immediately; it was the deck that had served them through their training whenever they had had some time to kill.

"Let's play some Euchre," Newton said.

"Shit, I got Benson," Williams groaned, realizing that he was sitting opposite Dennis at the table.

"That's news. I thought you had a wife," Mullen said.

"Screw you, Mullen," Williams said and sipped beer from his glass.

Dennis stared at Williams, who took a more comfortable position in his seat and checked his phone to see if someone had called or texted. Williams had blond hair, deep blue eyes, and sexy all-American good looks that would have made Dennis gladly jump into bed with him. Not that Dennis would ever admit it, but he had had a major crush on Williams soon after he had enlisted in the Marines.

Williams was totally oblivious to Dennis' desire for him—he didn't even know Dennis was gay. Nobody knew, except Dennis' parents. Dennis had enlisted in the Marine Corps right after high school to "increase his masculinity," or so he'd rationalized at the time. To his great disappointment, the Marines hadn't made him straight, so he had decided to come out to his parents. Remembering that awkward discussion a year ago still made him cringe.

"Mom, Dad, there is something I need to tell you," he said to his parents.

"What is it, honey?" his mother asked.

"What you just said about grandchildren...," Dennis hesitated. *"I'm gay."* He was worried that his parents would not take it well, but he just could not keep it inside him any longer.

"What did you just say?" his father said, dropping his fork and knife on the table.

"I said I'm gay," Dennis said, getting his confidence back. Both his parents were silent for a long time.

"Your mother and I never approved of your decision to join the Marines, but all these years, we have tried to understand," his father said, glaring at Dennis.

"It's my life, and I can do whatever I want with it," Dennis said, agitated.

"And this is my house, where you are no longer welcome," his father said harshly.

"You can't mean that," Dennis breathed in surprise.

"It's your life, Dennis. If you choose to whore around with other men instead of having a family, I'm not going to

watch it," his father said. "And don't expect me or your mother to approve of such a lifestyle," he added.

Before his mother could open her mouth, Dennis stood up and rushed out of the house, leaving the half-eaten Christmas Eve dinner on his plate.

That had been the last time he had eaten her cooking, and it had been his last visit to his childhood home where he had grown up playing and fighting with the neighborhood kids. That night, Dennis had decided to apply for Special Operations.

"You trying to stare a hole in Williams' chest?" Mullen taunted, waking Dennis from his thoughts.

"Um … it's just that picture on his shirt. AK-47, right? It was kind of cool to try the Kalashnikov in foreign weapons training," Dennis said.

"Huh? That Russian toy gun," Newton scoffed. "It's older than my gramma."

"You remember that guy, Hummel or something? He was so jazzed up about those guns that he almost peed in his pants," Mullen said. Everybody laughed.

"I heard he was expelled later," Williams said. "Mental issues, I guess," he added.

"Yeah, you gotta have some serious mental issues to join the military," Mullen and Newton said simultaneously.

Dennis laughed at the comment. He was one big mental case—or, like his mother had called him: a young rebel. While the other kids had played basketball on the street, Dennis had been persistent in asking until his father had given up and taken him to football training camp, even thought his father felt it was waste of money, which they did not have. In high school, the other kids had offered him the role of QB, out of respect or fear, but Dennis had wanted to play defensive line. He'd liked that it gave him more opportunities to tackle the opposing players. Besides, even though he had been the opinion leader in the locker room, he hadn't wanted to take the leading role in the game.

Mullen and Newton won the card game, which meant that Dennis and Williams offered the next round of beers. When the cute bartender arrived with their glasses, Dennis had a hard time not staring at him. Reluctantly, he turned his head and saw that there were quite a few customers in the bar. All of them seemed to be Marines, which was not a surprise since they were near Camp Pendleton in a neighborhood filled with houses for military personnel. Dennis had lived there for two years, and it was just starting to feel like home.

"Not the best place to pick up a chick," Newton said, looking around.

"You should try your luck with some of the guys over there," Mullen said, nodding toward a table on the other side of the room.

Dennis turned to look at the guys, obviously Marines even though they were not dressed in uniforms, and recognized one of them. He flinched when he realized that he had fooled around with the guy a couple of months ago in a cheap motel off I-15 near San Diego. The bastard had lied about being a bookkeeper who just happened to exercise at the gym regularly, not that Dennis had told him he was a Marine either. He should have known the guy was lying—nobody developed abs like that typing on a keyboard all day long. Maybe he had known but didn't really care. Maybe the story about being straight and wanting to experiment a little was a lie as well. Their eyes met, and both of them glanced away.

"I need to take a leak," Dennis said and rose from the table.

I should be more careful, he thought as he stepped into the restroom. He walked to the urinal and unzipped his pants, avoiding the temptation to take a quick peek at the equipment of the young guys to either side. Instead, he just stared at his own penis and hoped that the cute guy on his left would find it interesting. Unfortunately, he did not pay any attention to Dennis.

Only after the guys had left did he realize how the pungent smell of urine stung his nose. It was again a reminder of how shallow and pathetic his life was becoming: a lonely Marine searching for sex in a dirty toilet. He looked at himself in the mirror while washing his hands and felt depressed. Sometimes he wished he could find someone to share his life, but he was too worried what his buddies would think if they found out he was gay. Having an actual relationship would increase that risk significantly.

When Dennis returned to the table, he saw that the gym maniac bookkeeper was gone.

"How are my pals doing?" Dennis said, reaching out to steady himself as he took a seat. His hand grasped Newton's strong shoulder, and Dennis enjoyed the feeling before he finally had to let go.

"We missed you so much," Newton said as he laid his arm on Dennis' shoulder.

"Um … I've got some big news for you guys," Williams said. Everybody turned to look at him. To Dennis' disappointment, Newton pulled his arm from his shoulder.

"Please don't tell us that you are leaving the Marines," Mullen said.

"No, it's not that," Williams said quickly and then paused. "Janet's pregnant."

"Wow," Dennis said. "Congratulations, I guess. Daddy," he added.

The other guys congratulated the soon-to-be father, too. Dennis looked at Williams but could not tell what the expression on his face meant. He knew that Adler and Janet had met on some vacation trip in Honolulu two years ago and the couple had gotten married, quite suddenly, last summer. He felt a spike of jealousy in his chest when he realized that the child meant that the hot guy was out of his reach for good, not that he'd had high hopes of seducing a married straight guy, except in his fantasies. The news also reminded him that his teammates were moving on with their lives.

"I don't think I'd be ready to be a dad," Dennis said honestly, and then snapped his mouth shut, surprised that he'd said it aloud.

"As far as I know, you don't even have a girlfriend," Mullen said.

"You need a girl to make children?" Dennis said.

"Well, it helps, smartass," Mullen said. "I bet you've tried to make babies with Newton," he added and laughed.

"Maybe we should stop trying. Apparently it's not working," Dennis said to Newton, who punched him in the side.

"Toast for the daddy-to-be," Mullen said and raised his glass. Dennis took his glass and looked at Williams, who seemed to be unusually quiet.

They spent another hour in the bar, talking about all the funny things that had happened to them during the recon training, before they decided call it a day. On their way to the door, Newton grabbed Dennis' butt, grinned, and wished him good night. Dennis did the same to Newton, who did not mind Dennis touching him back. Well, he had started it. Besides, even if they had not been drunk, they were so used to physical contact because of the combat and martial arts training that it was hardly an issue. That was yet another reason Dennis loved the Marine Corps.

The sun had set, and the streetlights were illuminating the California night. The neighborhood felt peaceful, with the silence broken only by the occasional sound of cars as people returned from an evening shift. A small airplane was approaching the Oceanside Municipal Airport, which was a bit odd at that time of night.

Dennis walked back home, thinking of his dad's words about whoring around. *If that's what he expects of me, then that's what he'll get*, he thought acidly as he went to his bedroom to fetch his laptop. He opened the lid and logged in to the dating site. One particular new profile got his attention, and he had just started to browse the pictures when a pop-up appeared on the screen. He looked at the clock on the wall; it was half-past ten on Friday night.

By eleven, he was sitting in the backseat of a cab on his way to Carlsbad.

"Going on a date?" the driver asked. His accent indicated that he was a Mexican.

"Something like that," Dennis said.

"'Something like that,'" the driver repeated. "That's what I thought," he said and laughed.

"What do you mean?" Dennis asked.

"Nothing," the driver said. "I just drove two Marines to that address Saturday night. Must be quite a lady," he chuckled.

"I can hardly wait," Dennis said, mostly to himself, and suddenly he was not so sure if this trip had been a good idea after all.

Chapter 2

The loud voice of the muezzin calling for prayer from the nearby minaret of the Main Mosque woke Jafar Badri and his younger brother Rabih. They stood up, repeated the affirmation that there is no god but Allah, and finally bowed to glorify Him. Reciting the Kalimah had been part of the routine in the family as long as Jafar could remember, and he did not want to upset his father by neglecting this obligation. When the prayer was over, Rabih left the room, hiding his morning wood.

Jafar was 21 years old, single, and lived in his parents' house. His father was a manager at Nile Commercial Bank, which made it possible for the family to have a nice house in the district of Hai Jalaba in Juba. Unlike in many other districts in the capital of South Sudan, one did not witness an armed robbery or undernourished children lying dead on the streets every week, which made Hai Jalaba a popular place to live among the upper middle class.

The family lived a simple life. Like most wives in the neighborhood, Jafar's mother stayed at home and took care of the children and the household. Had they lived in America, she would have been called a housewife. In Sudan's patriarchal society, such titles did not exist, and any external observer, not familiar with the local culture, may have mistaken her for a hired servant.

"I'm done. The washing place is all yours," Rabih said when he returned to the bedroom.

"Thanks," Jafar yawned as he took his soap bar from the closet.

In the backyard of their house was a ragged bowl by a water container, and Jafar used it to clean himself quickly before he would go back inside for the breakfast his mother was preparing in the kitchen. It had not rained lately, but Jafar's younger sisters had brought water from the water station near the mosque to fill the container so that the men in the family could wash themselves before they left for work or school.

Jafar's older brother Abdul was a banker like his father, which created a tight bond between father and son. Jafar had had different plans, and his father had been furious when Jafar had told him that he would like to study at the Juba College of Nursing and Midwifery. Finally, his father had authorized it, but it was clear to both of them that his father would never respect that choice. In his eyes, Jafar would always be the one who broke the family tradition.

"*Al-hamdu lillah,*" Jafar said when he entered the small kitchen and saw his father.

The family waited until Mr. Badri had taken his place, and then they followed the example and sat on their pillows around the table. Jafar's mother and sisters had set tea, vegetables, and kisra bread on the table. Most families in South Sudan did not have enough money for breakfast, and Mr. Badri reminded them how grateful they should be for the wealth that Allah had blessed them with. Jafar looked at his father's big belly and could not help smiling as he silently praised the Lord.

"*Bismillahi wa 'ala baraka-tillah,*" everybody chorused, and then they started to eat.

After breakfast, Jafar's mother and sisters took the dishes and went to the backyard to wash them. Jafar, Rabih, and their father sat down on the chairs in the living room, which was the room where Jafar's sisters slept. They had already collected their mattresses from the floor so that the men could meet there.

"Jafar, I want you to drive Rabih to school today," Mr. Badri said.

"Yes, sir," Jafar said.

"But, Father, I can easily walk there," Rabih said, surprised that he was suddenly offered a ride.

"No," Mr. Badri said. "Some terrorists shot two people near the school yesterday. Jafar will drive you."

Life in Juba had become more and more dangerous since the ethnic violence worsened two years ago. It had begun with some clashes between the Murle and Nuer tribes in the state of Jonglei, but the conflict had recently escalated to plague the entire country. Over 10,000 people had been killed in the conflict intended to end with the genocide of the Nuer tribe.

"Let's go," Jafar said to his brother.

"And, Jafar, we have a family meeting today. Your uncle and cousin are coming. I want you at home by six," Mr. Badri said.

"Yes, sir," Jafar said.

Jafar took the keys, opened the front door, and sat down on the front seat of his 1998 Toyota Corona his father had bought him. He stretched himself over the passenger seat and pummeled the handle until the right front door opened. Abdul had suggested many times that Jafar should fix the handle outside the door, but he was too embarrassed to admit that he did not know how to fix it. Abdul, naturally, excelled at fixing cars—and at every other male work Jafar could think of.

The neighborhood was waking up to life. People were driving to work, dogs were barking here and there, and the chickens in their neighbor's yard made quite a fuss when Mrs. Alraheem captured one and cut its throat with a big knife. The smell of trash and dead animals was hovering everywhere, and the midday heat would only make it worse.

"You think Dad will let me play football on Sunday?" Rabih said when they were sitting in the car.

"I suppose it should be safe by then," Jafar said, even though he had no idea how the situation would evolve after the previous day's attack.

"No. I mean because Bastien and Corin are coming, too," Rabih said.

"Oh," Jafar said and was silent for a moment. "Don't tell Dad that they are Christians," he advised at last.

They drove along May Street, evading the biggest holes that the ongoing battles had left on the surface of the road. When they turned left on Unity Avenue, Jafar saw a group of armed men in front of the hospital. He drove one block, turned left again, and drove as fast as he could until they reached Juba Market at the other end of the street. He stopped the car and breathed rapidly. He had seen gunmen before, but never this close to their home.

"Should we try Lanya Street?" Jafar asked, scared.

"If you think it's safe," Rabih answered in a small voice.

"I don't know, but we can't stay here," Jafar said when they heard gunshots behind them.

People were running and screaming as the armed men were approaching the market area. Jafar turned left down a small and bumpy road and did his best to avoid hitting people who were desperately searching for a hiding place. Soon, they found their way to Lanya Street and turned right toward Supiri Secondary School. Once they got there, Jafar drove as close to the front door as he could, and his brother ran inside the school holding his bag to cover his head.

Jafar continued to Happy Street, though he did not feel cheerful, and scanned the area for any sign of further danger. Only when he arrived in the town district of Hai-Amarat did he feel safe. Most of the ministries and other government buildings were there, and even though those were potential targets for terrorism, Hai-Amarat was the best-guarded area in Juba. Jafar's work place, the US Embassy, was located there, too.

It was at the College of Nursing and Midwifery where Jafar had met an American girl from Florence Western Medical Clinic. She had told Jafar about her life in Los Angeles, and ever since then Jafar had had a dream: to move to America. He had almost asked his father to start organizing his marriage with the girl's parents, but she had told him that people in America made their own choices about marriage. That freedom felt tempting to Jafar.

Moving to America was a dream, and in South Sudan, most dreams were not meant to become real. Jafar knew that, realistically speaking, he had no hope of leaving the country. Even if he sold everything he owned, he could not afford a flight ticket to the US, especially not now when Juba International Airport was closed for civil flights because of the conflict and the closest international airport was in Ethiopia. To get as close to his dream as possible, Jafar had applied for a job in the US Embassy.

Jafar parked his car on Bowker Boulevard in front of the European Commission building and walked to the gates of the US Embassy. The parking area inside the fence was reserved for the ambassador and high-ranking officials. He showed his ID card at the gate and waited until the guard opened the heavy gate. Then he stepped into his paradise, heard the gate close behind him, and felt how the air was easier to breathe on American soil. To Jafar, it was worth going against his father's will.

"Good morning," Jafar said and smiled shyly to the janitor who was cleaning the parking lot.

"I'll come soon to fix the faucet in your coffee room," the janitor answered, and pointed toward the medical center where Jafar was walking.

"Thanks. That's great," Jafar said as he smiled at the man one more time and opened the front door.

The medical center was a small building opposite the main building where the ambassador had his office and private residence. It was clean, with white walls and air conditioning that made it comfortable to work there despite the blazing hot weather outside. Of course, Jafar was used to the heat, but he had noticed that the Americans appreciated the cool air inside. He walked to the room where the reception desk was located to check the schedule for the day and was surprised to find Ambassador Robert Witt waiting there.

"Morning, sir. How are you? How can I help you?" Jafar said politely.

"Morning, Jafar," the ambassador said in a friendly tone. "I wanted to check my vaccination status. Think you could help me?"

"Sure, sir. This way, please," Jafar said, amazed that the ambassador knew his name. He guided the ambassador to an empty room.

It was early morning, and aside from the cleaning ladies, no other employees had arrived yet. Jafar booted up the computer and started to search the ambassador's vaccination records. It took quite a while because the security policy forbade any local copies of data and Jafar had to download the records from the US over a highly secured connection. Before it was finished, the ambassador's cellphone started to ring.

"Robert Witt," the ambassador answered the phone. Jafar could not hear what the caller said, but the ambassador's face went serious.

"General Boyd, did I understand correctly that you just asked me to start evacuating the embassy?" the ambassador said and waited for a confirmation from the caller.

"Sir, I hope you understand that I need to confirm this with the State Department before I can start taking any actions," the ambassador said.

Jafar waited until the ambassador had asked several more questions and finally ended the call. The call lasted almost ten minutes, and the entire time Jafar was afraid that this would be his last day in paradise.

"That was US Special Operations Command. The commander himself," the ambassador said, still confused, before he realized that maybe he should not share the details with a nurse.

"Do we close the embassy?" Jafar asked, afraid of what the ambassador might answer.

"Not entirely, but we will limit the staff to minimum for the time being," the ambassador said.

"What about the medical center? I would like to stay," Jafar said quickly and looked at the ambassador like a puppy.

The ambassador smiled at Jafar's enthusiasm. He walked to the window and looked out, thinking what to do. He still had to confirm the evacuation with his supervisor in the Department of State, but he knew that the commander of the USSOCOM had not called him just to make a practical joke.

"Okay. I need at least one nurse at the medical center. Maybe it's good that you are local," the ambassador said.

"Thanks, sir," Jafar said and smiled widely.

"Is it okay for you to live in here, in the temporary apartments, during the evacuation?" the ambassador asked. "At least most of the time," he added.

"Sure, sir, that's okay," Jafar said, not sure what his father would think about that.

Just as Mr. Badri had been upset about Jafar's decision to become a nurse instead of a banker, he hadn't been particularly pleased when Jafar got a job at the embassy.

The difference was that, by the time Jafar got the job, their relationship had already become so distant that Mr. Badri did not care what his son did. What he did not know was that Jafar had never told those in the embassy that his family were Muslims. If his father ever learned Jafar had told his co-workers he was Christian, he knew he would be dead without any discussion about proper funerals.

"A group of Marines will arrive soon to protect the embassy during the evacuation," the ambassador said. "Can you start organizing their medical checks?"

"Of course. When do they arrive?" Jafar said.

"Next week, just after Christmas," the ambassador said.

"Fine, I'll make everything ready for them," Jafar said.

"Thanks, Jafar, I appreciate your help," the ambassador said, and smiled.

Jafar was enthusiastic. A group of young Americans would soon arrive in the embassy, and he would have a chance to live in the embassy with them. If he was lucky, he might be able to make friends with some of them. He was also happy that the ambassador knew his name and was so friendly. Maybe the ambassador could someday help him get to America.

"Sir, your vaccination," Jafar said when the ambassador was about to open the door to leave.

"Oh, I forgot it already," the ambassador said and returned. "I am starting to get old. I guess it really is time for me to retire."

"When are you retiring?" Jafar asked, taking the syringe from the cabinet.

"In April. I have only four months left. My wife and I have already bought a nice house in Florida," the ambassador said.

"Sounds nice," Jafar said, trying to hide his disappointment. The ambassador would leave, and he would stay.

Feeling frustrated, Jafar gave the ambassador the shot.

Chapter 3

The Williams lived in a nice wooden house that painted a light brown that looked almost pink to Dennis. A group of small trees was growing in front of the house, blocking the direct view from the street to the bedroom windows. The backyard was big and sunny, which made it perfect for barbequing, but Dennis found it a bit too empty. Maybe the Williams would get a swing set for their baby or something.

"Merry Christmas," Dennis said and gave the flowers to Janet, who had come to open the door for him.

"Thanks, Dennis. Come in," she said. "Adler's in the living room."

Sergeant Adler Williams and his wife Janet had invited Dennis for Christmas Eve dinner after they had heard that he did not have other plans. Dennis was grateful for the invitation. The memory of his father asking him to leave in the middle of Christmas dinner a year ago, just after Dennis had come out to them, was still too painful, and he had no intention of spending this Christmas with his parents—not that he had received an invitation from them.

There was a sweet smell of Christmas inside the house. Janet, who could no longer hide the coming baby, had apparently been baking and cooking, and Adler had set up a big Christmas tree in the living room. Dennis offered to help Janet in the kitchen, but she kindly declined and suggested that the men wait on the patio until dinner was ready.

"You still haven't made up with your parents?" Adler said, offering Dennis a bottle of beer.

"Huh … no," he said, feeling uncomfortable.

"Do you mind me asking what happened?" Adler said tentatively. They had never really talked about the topic.

"Old stuff. I don't want to talk about it," Dennis said and smiled weakly at his friend. He knew that Adler meant well.

"Okay, but I'll be here if you want to talk someday," Adler said.

Adler had noticed that something was wrong when Dennis had returned to Camp Pendleton after the Christmas holidays a year ago. Dennis, who typically was talking and joking all the time, had suddenly been serious and silent, spending a lot of time alone. Adler had tried to ask about it, but all Dennis had told him was that he had had an argument with his parents. They had never talked about it again, and then both men had joined the Training Company and gradually Dennis got his good mood back.

"I wonder when they'll assign us our first mission," Adler said when they settled on the patio chairs.

"I'm sure our turn to rescue to world will come soon," Dennis said and took a sip from his beer. "What does Janet think about all this? Baby coming and everything."

"She married a Marine," Adler said, like that explained everything.

"So, she knows that our missions can take several months? And if the shit hits the fan, we might never get back," Dennis said.

"If you ever find a girl, that's one of the first conversations you need to have with her," Adler said.

Dennis looked at Adler and thought about what he had just said. Dennis had never dated anyone, not even in high school, despite the social pressure. The one-night hook-ups had made it possible to live a life where he did not have to make any commitments and, more importantly, could keep his sexual orientation hidden. The problem was that, the older he got, the more he wanted to settle down.

"I heard that Mullen's bringing his girlfriend to his parents' house for dinner tomorrow," Adler said.

"The new blonde? Wow. That's getting serious," Dennis said and smiled.

"So, it's only you and Newton who are not dating," Adler said.

"Yeah, he's not my type," Dennis said, knowing Adler would take it as a joke. It was a lie: Newton was his type for sure.

Adler laughed, just like Dennis had assumed. Dennis used these jokes to test how Adler would react if he knew the truth about him but, unfortunately, Adler seemed not to understand the hints. It was frustrating, but at least he'd never started any gay rant either when Dennis made jokes about gays.

"I hope she's properly dressed. Mullen's father is such a patriot," Dennis said.

"You remember that mini-skirt?" Adler said, and Dennis nodded. "It was hot as hell, but he might not appreciate it."

"I've met the old man only once, but all he talked was about God, family values, and how the Democrats have ruined the country," Dennis said.

"I can imagine," Adler said and laughed.

"God bless the United States of America." Dennis raised his bottle.

Just as he said it, Janet appeared at the patio door and rolled her eyes. A delicious smell of freshly cooked food was wafting from the kitchen. She invited the men to the table and waited until both of them had finished their beers.

They walked in, and Dennis stopped when he saw the table. The lights in the dining room were dimmed, and there were three candles that lit the table and created a romantic atmosphere. A vase full of white roses was centered on the table, which was covered with a red tablecloth.

"This really should be a dinner for two," Dennis said, feeling like a third wheel.

"Nonsense, we both wanted to invite you," Janet said honestly when she saw the expression on Dennis' face.

"Are you sure? This looks so beautiful," Dennis said.

"Thanks, Dennis. I'm happy that at least somebody recognizes it," Janet said and gave her husband a meaningful look.

"Yeah, Dennis is the romantic guy," Adler teased, "and I'm the one who is married."

Dennis was used to Adler giving him a hard time. It was not the first time Adler had called him romantic, even though typically Adler's comments were related to his obsession with his hair. Dennis' hair was short, like most of the Marines', but he still spent a lot of time making sure it looked perfect.

"I'm sure Dennis will be married soon, too. Right?" Janet said to Dennis after they had sat down at the table.

"Um ... I'm still looking for the right one," Dennis said. He felt uncomfortable, and Janet must have noticed it.

"I'm so excited about the baby," Janet said quickly, changing the topic. "Adler will be a great dad," she added and looked at her husband.

"Yeah, sure," Adler said.

For a moment, Dennis thought he saw some change in Adler's body language. It was like the tiniest hint that something was wrong. Then it was gone, and they started to eat.

Janet had cooked an assortment of different food, which all looked delicious to Dennis. Spread across the table were a big turkey, roasted beef, potato casserole, carrots, two different salads, and homemade garlic bread. They did their best but could eat only a small portion of the food. As if that had not been enough, Janet brought out a big cake for dessert, which made the men roll their eyes.

"Are you trying to kill us with all this food?" Adler said.

"C'mon, it's Christmas," Janet said and kissed Adler on the cheek before she returned to her place at the table.

"Oh, shit," Dennis said. "Sorry about the language, but this cake's so good."

"Yet another point for the romantic guy," Adler said.

Dennis smiled at the comment. He felt lucky that he had friends like Adler and Janet, who had invited him over for dinner instead of spending some quality time together. The four-person reconnaissance team could be assigned a mission at any time, which would mean that Adler could spend weeks or months away from home. For the Marines in a special operations company, any time with family and friends was luxury that could not be taken for granted.

"Thanks, Janet, the dinner was perfect," Dennis said after finishing his third or fourth piece of the cake.

"I'm glad that you liked it," she said, beaming.

"Liked it?" Dennis said. "I loved it, very passionately."

Adler rose from his seat. "Dennis is a very passionate lover," he said and patted Dennis on the shoulder.

Indeed, Dennis thought and stared at Adler maybe a little bit too long.

"Let's go to the living room. The chairs there are more comfortable, and I've got some whiskey in the cabinet," Adler said.

The three of them spent a nice evening together. Dennis liked Janet a lot. Adler had been very lucky to find her, and he could not remember when he'd last laughed so much. All too soon, not only was the whiskey empty, but Dennis had to leave. Janet had offered to let him sleep in their guest room, but he felt that it would have been too much.

Dennis opened the front door and looked at the neighborhood. There were lights on all the houses, and the happy families were celebrating the Christmas Eve. It reminded Dennis of his parents.

"Thanks for the visit. It was great to have you here," Adler said.

"No. Thank you for inviting me," Dennis said.

"And if you ever want to talk about your parents…," Adler said.

"Someday you might hear the whole story," Dennis said, knowing that that day might not never come. Then he thanked Adler one more time and left.

The next morning, Dennis woke when he heard some loud noise coming from very close. It took a while for him to realize that it was his cellphone, which was ringing. He took the phone and was surprised to notice that it was his mother who was calling him.

"Hi, Mom," he answered tentatively.

"Merry Christmas, Dennis," she said. Her voice was not cheerful, but it sounded cautious.

"Thanks … you, too," he said, not sure if he meant it. He was still feeling the effects of the whiskey from the night before.

"Um … how're you doing?" she asked.

"I'm fine. I've got some good friends who invited me for dinner yesterday," he said, not even trying to hide the bitterness in his voice.

"That's nice," she said.

After a long pause, they continued the awkward discussion for a while. She asked simple questions, and Dennis gave short answers. Dennis was not ready to forgive his mother for rejecting him a year ago, but it still felt good to talk with her. Gradually he became more cooperative, and even though she did not say it aloud, he sensed that she had called to apologize.

"Could I talk with Dad, too?" Dennis said.

"Um … he's not here right now," she said, and Dennis knew she was lying.

"He doesn't want to talk to me," he said. It was more like a statement than a question.

"No, he doesn't…. Look, he needs more time," she added quickly.

"I don't have time for him," he said and hung up.

She did not try to call him again, and soon Dennis started to regret that he had ended the call so suddenly. After all, it was the first time in a year that he had talked with either of his parents. What made him angry and frustrated was that she had not made a single attempt to say she was sorry. She had just called him and started asking how he was doing like nothing had ever happened.

Maybe she was not even sorry, Dennis thought. *Maybe she still thinks that I chose to be gay, just to embarrass them.*

The call with his mother and the thoughts it raised made him upset. He ran his fingers though his hair, frustrated that his parents were such donkeys, and decided he need to take his mind off them. He took his laptop and navigated to a gay porn site where young guys were showing their cocks to a webcam. He browsed a couple of rooms before he found the one with the two Columbian boys he had been watching earlier. Then he slipped out of his boxers and jerked off. It did not take long before he got the phone call with his mother out of his mind.

The day after Christmas, Adler called Dennis, who hardly got a chance to say a word before Adler told him that he was coming over. As instructed, Dennis opened the wardrobe in his bedroom to find some nice clothes. He was happy that he had taken a shower some hours ago because Adler had not given him much time to prepare. Fifteen minutes later, he was sitting in Adler's car.

"Where are we going?" Dennis said as Adler started to drive.

"To Carlsbad," Adler said mysteriously.

Adler turned up the volume when the radio station started to play some megahit from The Rasmus. Dennis could not remember the name of the song even though his favorite gay club in LA had played the song each time he had taken a vacation from his heterosexual bubble and visited the LA gay scene. He started to sing along and noticed that they had already left the suburbs and were driving on the highway.

"When are you gonna tell me where we're going?" Dennis said.

"I'm taking you to a bar. It's time to find you a girl," Adler said. "Actually, it was Janet's idea," he admitted.

"Oh," Dennis said, and kept his eyes on the road ahead. *Highway to hell*, he thought.

The closer to Carlsbad they got, the more nervous Dennis became. For a short time, he considered confessing to Adler that he was gay, but whenever he opened his mouth to blurt it out, no words came out.

41

"It's the day after Christmas," Dennis said weakly, realizing how ridiculous it sounded. "Are you sure there are any bars open?"

"I checked on the Internet. They're all open, and one even has a special program for singles," Adler said.

"Huh? What's that?" Dennis said.

"I don't know. Blind dating or something, I guess," Adler said.

Dennis sighed. The night was turning into a nightmare. Soon he was expected to date girls, and his team leader would be monitoring the event and doing his best to pair him with some desperate girl who had come there to hunt a man for herself. It was not hard for Dennis to imagine the predators lurking there.

"Um … would you mind if we went to see a movie or something instead?" Dennis asked tentatively. "I don't feel like dating today."

"A movie? You wanna see a movie with me instead of dating a girl," Adler joked. "Are you gay or something?" he added and laughed loudly.

Dennis blushed and did not know what to say. The opportunity to come out had been offered to him on a silver plate, but Dennis hesitated too long. Adler was too focused on the traffic to notice anything.

"Okay. Let's go to a movie," Adler said before Dennis could decide whether to answer Adler's question.

When they arrived in Carlsbad, they checked a couple of movie theaters before they found one that was open. It was a small theater in an old building. On the left next to the front doors was a sign explaining that it was the first theater in Carlsbad and was established in 1962. They walked into the entrance hall, which was small, dark, and smelled old.

"Welcome, gentlemen," a gray-haired lady greeted them behind the counter. "The movies started ten minutes ago, but I'll let you in if you hurry."

"Thanks," Adler said. "What's playing today?"

"There's a war movie and a romantic comedy." The old lady studied them. "I guess you want to see the war movie," she said as she started to walk toward the door that led to the bigger auditorium.

"Actually, we would prefer the comedy," Dennis interrupted. They saw enough war at their work.

"As you wish, darling," she said and opened the door to the smaller auditorium.

Just when they stepped in, she looked at them once again, smiled, and winked at Dennis. Then she closed the door behind them, and Dennis and Adler took seats in the back row. There were only three other couples sitting in the dark auditorium, and one of them was more focused on each other than the movie.

The seats were narrow, and Dennis could feel Adler's shoulder and leg against his. He enjoyed the closeness and the warmth that was radiating from Adler, and he resisted the temptation to put his hand on Adler's leg. He knew that he was as close to his dream boy as he could ever be.

It felt good and bitter at the same time, and caused some stirring in his crotch.

All too soon, the movie ended, and they returned to their cozy suburb near Camp Pendleton. The sun had set already, and it was unexceptionally silent there. They drove to Adler's house and found Janet watching television in the living room.

"You're early. Did you find Dennis a wife already?" Janet said, smiling.

"Actually, he wanted to see a movie with me," Adler said, emphasizing the last two words.

"Well, you are a good man, but you're taken," Janet said and giggled.

"Did you say something about eggnog?" Dennis said to Adler, wanting to change the subject.

"Sit down. I'll make you some," Janet said and left to the kitchen.

Dennis watched as Janet disappeared to the kitchen, and he thought about what a good wife Adler had found. It was not that Adler expected her to serve him all the time; actually, it had first made him feel uncomfortable. Then he had realized that Janet really enjoyed cooking and pampering him, and he had started to contribute to the housework by cleaning and taking care of the yard.

They sat together talking and drinking the eggnog until Janet said that she was tired and was going to bed. The men took a half-full whiskey bottle and moved to the patio so they would not disturb her.

"I need to tell you something," Adler said after his third or fourth glass. "But you have to promise not to tell Janet," he added and looked Dennis directly in the eyes.

"I won't tell," Dennis said, waiting for what his teammate would tell him.

"This is embarrassing," Adler started and hesitated a while. "I'm not ready to become a father," he blurted out.

"You didn't plan it together?" Dennis said, surprised. Adler shook his head.

They sat in a silence for a while. Dennis was struggling to find a way to respond to what Adler had just said. The idea of having children of his own felt distant to him, and he had a hard time relating to Adler's position.

"I even thought that we should get an abortion," Adler said.

"Oh," Dennis said.

"But Janet is so excited. There is no way I could propose something like that," Adler said.

"I see," Dennis murmured.

"Am I a bad person to think about … that?" Adler asked.

Dennis didn't know how to answer. He wanted to comfort Adler by hugging him, but he was afraid that Adler would take it the wrong way. Instead, he patted Adler on his back and told him that everything would be fine. Then he saw that Janet had appeared at the patio door holding Adler's cellphone in her hand. Dennis felt a moment of panic for Adler that she had heard their discussion. Apparently she hadn't as she kept smiling at the men.

"It's your boss calling," she said. "I told him that you might be a bit drunk," she added and rolled her eyes.

Adler took the phone from Janet and answered. It was a short conversation, and after it finished, he looked at Janet and then Dennis.

"We're going to Africa on Monday," he said. "To protect the US Embassy in South Sudan," he added.

"For how long? And why are they sending a recon team to protect an embassy instead of an embassy guard team from Quantico?" Dennis asked.

Adler raised his hands. He had no answers. They were a special operations team trained to complete very different kinds of missions, and this did not make much sense.

Chapter 4

Jafar had fulfilled Ambassador Robert Witt's request and had moved to an apartment in the embassy over the weekend. His father had hardly said a word when he had announced his moving plans. Jafar had emphasized that it was only a temporary arrangement and that he would live with the Americans only as long as the evacuation took place, but it didn't matter.

"Do whatever you want," his father had said before he spat on the floor and left Jafar standing alone in the living room.

It was Monday evening, and Jafar was standing in front of the medical center, aware that his absence from home would annoy his father. It bothered him, but on the other hand, he was eagerly waiting for the Marines to arrive. He forced his father out of his mind when he saw the gates open and a military vehicle drive in to park in front of the main building. Four Marines stepped out and looked around.

"Welcome to the embassy. I'm Robert Witt," the ambassador said when he walked from the main building to shake hands with the Marines.

"Sergeant Adler Williams," Jafar heard one of the Marines introducing himself.

Jafar's focus was, however, on the dark-haired Marine that was standing behind Sergeant Williams. He could not explain why, but something in the Marine's face made it difficult for him to stop staring. When the Marine noticed his gaze, Jafar panicked and escaped into the medical center. He almost walked right into Doctor Baldwin, who was the Medical Director.

"We are leaving now. Will you be okay?" Doctor Baldwin said.

The evacuation flight for the medical center employees was scheduled for the same evening. During the forthcoming weeks, Jafar would be working there alone.

"I'll be fine. Have a safe journey," Jafar said, still feeling confused.

"If you have problems and need help, you can call Doctor Lienert at the embassy in Ethiopia," Doctor Baldwin said.

"Huh? Sure, thanks," Jafar replied and said goodbye to the rest of his colleagues before he started to organize things for next day.

Performing medical checks for the Marines was mostly a formality that the operating procedures required. The Reconnaissance Battalion had a military hospital at Camp Pendleton, which was capable of sending doctors and nurses all over the world wherever the teams were assigned. However, now that they had been boarded at the embassy, without their own medical team, the State Department took care of their health.

Jafar took the file that Doctor Baldwin had left and started to read the names of the Marines: Adler Williams, Dennis Benson, Ethan Mullen, and Brian Newton. The paperwork mentioned that they were a Force Recon Team and their mission was authorized by General Anthony Boyd, the Commander of the United States Special Operations Command. Jafar did not know what that meant, but it sounded exciting to him.

At eight o'clock, Jafar walked to the big cafeteria where supper was served. The room was almost empty; most of the employees had been evacuated already. Jafar took tea and some vegetables from the buffet table and noticed the Marines sitting at the table on the left. He hesitated a bit but then started to move in the same direction. He did not want to interrupt their discussion, so he set his teacup on an empty table near them.

"Do you work here?" someone asked. Jafar turned and noticed that it was the dark-haired Marine.

"You speak English?" the Marine said when Jafar did not say anything but just stared at them.

"Yes," Jafar said quickly. "And yes, I work here. I'm a nurse," he added shyly.

"Come and sit with us. We just arrived here," the Marine said. "I'm Dennis, by the way, and these jerks are my teammates," he added.

The rest of the Marines introduced themselves and continued eating their supper. Jafar listened silently, too nervous to say a word. He noticed that, most of the time, Dennis was leading the discussion, even though the other guys were quite talkative as well.

In America, people have so much to say, and they don't hesitate to share it with others, Jafar thought and stayed quiet.

"So, Jafar, was it? Where do you live?" Dennis asked out of the blue.

"Um … I live here at the embassy," Jafar said, confused by the sudden attention.

"You live here?" Dennis said and looked surprised.

"I mean I'm here during the evacuation. I live with my parents in Hai Jalaba," Jafar said.

"You live with your parents?" one of the Marines asked.

"My father has not arranged me a wife yet," Jafar said, embarrassed. The Marines looked at each other.

The Marines were interested in hearing more about Jafar's family and life in South Sudan. Jafar answered their questions politely, hoping that someday the Marines would tell him about their lives in the US. When the meal was over, Jafar offered to clean the table, but the Marines refused and cleared their own dishes.

The following morning, Dennis knocked on the door of the consulting room where Jafar was performing the medical checks for the Marines. He stepped in smiling and shook hands with Jafar. He was dressed in his civilian clothes and looked relaxed despite the long flight on the previous day.

"Could you please take off your shirt? I'll measure your heart rate and blood pressure," Jafar said and turned to take the equipment from the cabinet.

"Sure," Dennis said nonchalantly and started to undress.

"According to your records, you need a booster for the typhoid vaccination," Jafar said, looking at his papers.

"I'm a big boy. I can take it," Dennis said.

When Jafar turned, he almost dropped the blood pressure meter. Dennis was standing naked in front of him, and his body was lean and muscular. Jafar got a glimpse of Dennis' crotch before he quickly turned around.

"Um … the vaccination … it goes in your arm," Jafar said, nervously.

"Oh. At the base camp, they always poke those needles in my butt," Dennis said and took his boxers from the chair.

Jafar laughed nervously and started to wrap the blood pressure meter around Dennis' arm. His hands touched Dennis' skin, which increased his nervousness in a way that he could not explain. There was an awkward silence when the automatic meter started to fill the bag with air to take the measurements. Jafar did not know what to say or where to look.

"I'll give you the vaccination next, and then there are a couple of standard questions you need to answer," Jafar said when the measurement was complete.

"Okay," Dennis said and followed Jafar with his gaze.

It took some time for Jafar to find the right needle from the storage room. When he returned, Dennis was sitting in the consulting room still wearing only his boxers. He stretched his arms, almost as if he were presenting his muscles. Jafar did his best to look Dennis in his eyes when he explained how the vaccination would work.

"This might hurt a little," Jafar said as he held the needle close to the skin.

"Just go ahead," Dennis said. "Trust me; I've had much worse pain."

Dennis did not even twitch when Jafar pushed the needle through his skin and injected the vaccination in the muscle. Jafar gave Dennis a piece of gauze and asked him to press the place where he had given the vaccination. That would prevent the skin from bruising.

Doctor Baldwin had left Jafar the medical questionnaire that the doctors used to assess risks that might prevent the

Marines from taking part in military operations. They were all routine questions, and Dennis passed the test easily, which meant that the medical check was completed.

"Are you very busy, or can I ask you something?" Dennis asked when he was dressing.

"Sure you can," Jafar said.

"How's life in Juba?" Dennis said.

"The country gained independence just a couple of years ago," Jafar said. "Unfortunately the war began soon after."

"Why are they fighting?" Dennis asked.

"People haven't learned to live together. If you're different, you must die," Jafar said bluntly.

Jafar explained how the embassy had organized a couple of evacuation flights for foreigners living in South Sudan. Most of them had obviously been Americans who were in Juba for one reason or another. Four months ago, Jafar had helped a frightened family, and he had seen how they all cried when the armored military car had finally arrived to take them to the airport.

"How old are you?" Dennis asked.

"I'm twenty-one," Jafar said.

"And you said yesterday that your father is arranging you a wife? You cannot choose yourself?" Dennis said.

"We had a family meeting last week. I have a cousin who will soon be fourteen. My father's discussing the price with his brother," Jafar said.

Dennis' jaw dropped. He could not believe what he had just heard. Jafar explained how most of the marriages were organized and told him that people typically married someone from the same tribe, often even from the same family.

"Isn't she quite young?" Dennis said.

"Well, they say that Mary was even younger when Jesus was born," Jafar said and smiled.

"If you believe in that story," Dennis muttered to himself before raising his voice. "Do you even like her? I mean ... if your father has chosen her for you."

"I don't know her well, but I think I can learn to like her," Jafar said.

Jafar looked at his watch and apologized that he had to start preparing for the next check. He would have liked to continue his conversation with Dennis, now that he was not so nervous anymore, but Sergeant Williams would arrive soon.

"Wanna show me the city someday if we manage to get some spare time?" Dennis asked, holding his hand at the door handle, ready to step out.

"Um ... sure, that would be cool," Jafar said and smiled, maybe a bit too much.

"Great. See you later," Dennis said and left.

Not really sure of what had just happened, Jafar stood in the middle of the room and kept staring at the empty door where Dennis had stood only a moment ago. He was so lost in his own thoughts that Adler Williams almost scared him when he walked in.

The evacuation of the embassy was completed by Saturday morning, and Jafar got the chance to show Juba to Dennis after breakfast. Dennis dressed in civilian clothes since the Marine Corps combat utility uniform would have drawn unwanted attention and provoked violent behavior, especially when the other Marines were not there with him.

They were driving around the city center with Jafar pointing out the locations of government buildings. To Dennis, everything looked rather new but kind of cheap. Juba was one of the fastest growing cities in the world, thanks to foreign investments, but most of the buildings were low and had only one or two floors. Driving in the city was unpleasant since the roads were mostly unpaved, surfaced with gravel and very bumpy.

"What's that?" Dennis asked when they spotted a herd of cows crossing the town.

"They're on their way to the cattle market," Jafar said. "They sell the cows there."

"Yeah, I kind of assumed that," Dennis said, smiling.

They followed the cows to a vibrant market area, which was full of people selling the animals, local food, or handicrafts, or just spending time talking with other people. Two dozen *boda boda* motorbike taxis were parked on one edge of the market area in the shadows of the big trees.

"Wanna see the White Nile?" Jafar said after they had been watching the market a while.

"Sure," Dennis said, excited.

"Let's go then," Jafar said. "I need to be home by dinner time, but we have still plenty of time," he added.

"Another family meeting to arrange your marriage?" Dennis asked. Jafar nodded but did not look too eager to join this dinner.

They drove along Mboro Street and passed the University of Juba. After five miles, they arrived at the Juba Bridge and saw the longest river in the world. The water was surprisingly blue and clean; Dennis had expected it to be brown and full of garbage and dead fish.

"I'm starving. Let's go there," Dennis said and pointed at a restaurant on the riverbank.

"Um … it's a nice restaurant, but I don't have enough money," Jafar said, embarrassed. "You go, and I'll wait for you here."

"Nonsense. I'll pay," Dennis said and stepped out of the car.

"Wait. I can't let you pay. It's too much," Jafar said.

"Consider it payment for the sightseeing tour," Dennis said and continued walking toward the restaurant. Jafar followed him, still not convinced that he should let Dennis pay for him.

The waiter, who was the owner's brother, guided them to a nice table with an amazing view of the river. Dennis could not understand the menu, even though it was written in English, so they ended up ordering what the waiter recommended. The food was not as brilliant as the view, but they ate everything with good appetite.

"Anything for dessert, gentlemen?" the waiter asked after he had cleaned the table.

"Coffee for me, and my boyfriend will have a cup of tea," Dennis said. He meant it as a joke, but it was not well-received.

"Get out of the restaurant!" the waiter roared.

"But we haven't even—" Dennis said.

"Out! Now!" the waiter said and pushed them toward the door.

For a moment, Dennis considered fighting back, but soon he realized that it was better to just leave. Jafar was in shock and ran to the car as fast as he could. Dennis followed him, walking.

"Get in! We need to leave," Jafar said urgently. As soon as Dennis had sat down, he accelerated toward the town center.

"We need to try that again if we want to eat without paying," Dennis said, still amused.

"Are you crazy? You almost got us killed. The police might be there soon," Jafar said. He was still in panic.

"Police? Why?" Dennis said.

"You told him we are sodomites. That could lead to years in prison or a death sentence," Jafar said.

"Oh," Dennis said. "Sorry. I didn't know," he added, at a loss for what else to say.

They drove in silence, and Jafar was constantly looking at the rearview mirror to check whether somebody was following them. They passed the Hai-Malakal Cemetery and turned left to a dense residential area, which would provide them a good hiding place. After several turns, they finally stopped in a small parking area.

"Look, I'm really sorry. I didn't mean to—"

"It's okay," Jafar interrupted. He seemed to be a bit relaxed already. "Just don't do it again," he said.

"They don't seem to like gays here," Dennis said and laughed.

"It's a severe crime," Jafar said.

"That's what you think?" Dennis said, trying to determine Jafar's opinion on the matter.

"I don't know. I mean, it's a bit weird, but I don't think they harm other people," Jafar said.

Dennis stepped out of the car and walked to a nearby booth to buy coffee for himself and tea for Jafar. There was a small park on the other side of the parking area, and Dennis was able to convince Jafar that it was safe to get out of the car and walk there to enjoy their drinks. Besides, the big trees provided them shelter from the sun, unlike Jafar's Corona, which did not have any kind of air conditioning.

"Can you show me where you live?" Dennis asked after he had finished his coffee.

"Um … maybe we can drive there, but I can't take you in the house," Jafar said. "My father's there."

"He doesn't like Marines or Americans?" Dennis said.

"Neither, I guess," Jafar said, embarrassed.

When they were walking back to Jafar's car, his cellphone started to ring. The Chief of Staff had given him one when the evacuation started since Jafar was the only one working in the medical center. Jafar looked at the phone, puzzled, and Dennis had to show him how to answer it, which Jafar found a bit embarrassing. After the call, he told Dennis that they had to return to the embassy.

"Thanks for the tour. I had fun," Dennis said when they had parked the car.

"Me, too. Maybe we can go again someday," Jafar said and hoped that he did not sound too enthusiastic.

"Sure," Dennis said as he walked into the residence building where the Marines had their rooms. The embassy Chief of Staff stop him at the door.

"Soldier, why aren't you in uniform?" the Chief of Staff asked.

"I spent some spare time in the city," Dennis said. *Besides, I'm not a soldier.*

"Next time you might remember to inform me before you leave," the Chief of Staff said and left.

In the meanwhile, Jafar had entered the medical center and found Private Newton waiting in the lobby with an embassy worker from the ambassador's office. Newton sat on a chair; he was pale and shaking. Jafar helped Newton to the consulting room and called the US Embassy in Ethiopia. He hoped that Doctor Lienert was there and could help him.

Doctor Lienert was not in the embassy, but he returned Jafar's call fifteen minutes later. He sounded a bit irritated and asked Jafar to give the phone to Private Newton. They talked for a while, and then Doctor Lienert gave short instructions to Jafar.

Newton swallowed the pills that Jafar gave him, but as soon as he rose from the chair, he mumbled something and almost crashed to the ground. Jafar took quickly hold of him. The slender nurse had to use all his power to keep the big Marine from falling down. He struggled to pull Newton's arm around his shoulder and walked him to bed. Newton slept like a baby, totally oblivious that Jafar paced nervously around the medical center and checked every five minutes to make sure Newton was still breathing. In addition to Newton's condition, he was worried that he would be late for the family meeting.

"How is he?" Dennis asked when he arrived in the medical center two hours later.

"Sleeping, but he was awake a moment ago and feels much better now," Jafar said and looked at his watch. Dennis noticed it.

"Go and have dinner with your family," Dennis said. "I'll look after Newton."

"Are you sure?" Jafar asked, delighted.

"Yeah. Just give me your number. I'll call if something happens," Dennis said.

Jafar wrote his number on a piece of paper and changed his clothes rapidly. His father had made it clear that this dinner was important, and Jafar had an idea what would happen if he missed it. He ran to his car thinking that if there was not much traffic he would still be home on time. Unfortunately, there were many cars going in the same direction.

"Sit down," Mr. Badri said angrily when Jafar entered the kitchen ten minutes late.

"I'm sorry, Father. I had a patient," Jafar said.

"And we have a dinner," Mr. Badri said. "What could you do anyway? Don't the Americans have a doctor there?" he added.

Embarrassed, Jafar sat down next to his older brother and said the prayer. The others had already started to eat. Jafar's uncle, his wife, and their daughter sat on the pillows on the opposite side of the table.

"I've agreed with my brother that you'll marry his daughter, Amira," Mr. Badri said.

"Hi, Jafar," Amira said timidly and smiled at her future husband.

"My brother's building you a room onto their farmhouse. You can move there in a couple of weeks," Mr. Badri said.

"Okay," Jafar said.

"And one more thing. We agreed that you'll stop working for the Americans and help my brother at the farm," Mr. Badri said.

Jafar was shocked, and he looked at his father with his eyes full of terror. He knew that he was expected to live with his parents-in-law until they could afford a house of their own, but he was not prepared to quit his job at the embassy. Suddenly this whole marriage thing did not sound like a good idea at all. He was about to protest when his father gave him a warning look.

"Welcome to the family," Mr. Badri's brother said.

"Thanks," Jafar said disappointedly.

"We'll make you a good farmer," Jafar's uncle said nonchalantly, ignoring Jafar's discontent tone. "You'll just need some muscles first," he added, and everybody laughed, except Jafar.

After dinner, the women started to wash the dishes, and the men decided to go to the mosque. Jafar and Amira were excused from both activities. They moved to the living room where Jafar's mother served them a small dessert. He was sure that the parents had organized this to give them some time to get to know each other.

"I'm so excited to get married," Amira said and giggled.

"Me too," Jafar said. "And surprised," he added.

"Why's that?" Amira asked.

Jafar was about to tell her that, after the arguments about his education and workplace, he did not expect his father to arrange him a wife. Maybe he just wanted Jafar out of the house. He kept his thoughts to himself and lied to Amira, saying that he was surprised because everything had happened so fast.

"So, do you like me?" Amira asked, and smiled shyly.

"I think you're pretty," Jafar said.

"I've always dreamed of a big family. We can raise our children at my parents' farm," she said. "Would that be nice?" she asked hopefully.

"That sounds nice," Jafar said, having a hard time fitting a big family at his in-laws' farm into his dream of moving to America.

"I'm so happy that my father chose you to be my husband," she said, beaming.

They kept talking until the men returned from the mosque. Then Amira's family left, and Jafar drove back to the embassy. He washed his face in the sink and went straight to bed. The events of the day were replaying in his head and keeping him awake. *I'll be married soon, and become a farmer,* he thought before he finally fell asleep.

The following morning, Jafar woke up with a hard erection. He had been dreaming of Dennis, who had been naked in his dream. It made him feel confused and worried.

Chapter 5

The morning sun woke Dennis. Lazily, he rose from his bed, trying not to disturb Adler, who was still sleeping. Adler looked so innocent, but Dennis could not help entertaining the idea of peeking under his blanket. *God, I'm so horny*, he thought, and adjusted his boxers.

Dennis passed Jafar's room on his way to the shower room at the end of the corridor. The door to Jafar's room was half-open, and the room seemed empty. Dennis assumed that the cute nurse had already left for breakfast.

He must be gay. Everything in him is screaming that he is, Dennis thought, and found himself grinning. He was not sure how long he would have to spend in this rat hole, but he looked forward to having some fun with Jafar. The idea of having sex with Jafar made him hard, and he hoped that the other Marines would not catch him red-handed in the shower room.

After a quick shower, Dennis rushed to the canteen and was happy to spot Jafar there. Unfortunately, he was finishing his breakfast, so Dennis had to act quickly. He poured himself a cup of coffee and took it to the table where Jafar was sitting.

"Would you mind keeping me company, or are you busy?" Dennis said.

"Huh? I guess I'm not busy," Jafar said. Seeing Dennis reminded him of the dream that still confused him.

"So, what's up?" Dennis sipped coffee from the mug.

"Um … I saw my bride yesterday," Jafar said.

"How was she?" Dennis asked, not really interested in the answer. Actually, he was feeling a bit jealous.

"I think she was pretty," Jafar said.

Dennis studied Jafar carefully. Although Dennis might not fit to any stereotype himself, the slender nurse who was smiling sheepishly was the most feminine guy he had ever met, except the two transvestites he'd once talked with in a gay club in LA. Dennis had a hard time believing that Jafar was really into girls. He decided to play with the guy to check his reaction.

"Wanna go into town again next weekend?" Dennis asked.

"Well, I—" Jafar started, but Dennis interrupted him, leaning forward suddenly.

"I promise I won't tell anyone that you are my boyfriend," he whispered in Jafar's ear.

Jafar went silent. Dennis drank coffee from his mug nonchalantly and kept looking at Jafar, who was scratching his arms.

"I think I need to go," Jafar said, and rose from the table.

"I'm sorry. I was just joking," Dennis said, feeling like an idiot.

"It's okay," Jafar said and left.

Dennis watched him walking away. He would have wanted to run after Jafar and explain, but what could he have said? *Sorry, I know you're marrying a girl, but I just thought you were gay and decided to joke about it.* It did not sound like something Jafar would like to hear.

Disappointed, Dennis walked to the buffet table, filled another mug with coffee, and returned to his room with the coffee mugs and two croissants. He assumed that Adler would wake up soon and want some breakfast. He was surprised to find Adler standing in the room naked and drying his short hair with a towel when he opened the door.

"Thanks!" Adler said, delighted, when he saw what Dennis was carrying.

"I thought you would be hungry," Dennis said as he took a peek at Adler's crotch.

"Just a minute. I'll put some clothes on," Adler said.

Adler folded the towel on a seat back and walked naked to the other side of the small room to get some clean clothes from his bag. Dennis had seen Adler naked several times and always liked what he saw. He was strong and physically robust, bigger than Dennis, and definitely different from Jafar. Even as he tried not to stare at Adler, Dennis had to admit there was something in Jafar's looks that tempted him.

Once Adler had dressed, they started eating their breakfast, and Dennis told him about the trip to Juba with Jafar. He did not mention the accident at the restaurant; in fact, he lied and said he had me a girl at the restaurant.

"I'm jealous," Adler said.

"Of me? Why?" Dennis asked, surprised.

"You're single and free to go and have fun. Soon I'll be stuck at home, changing diapers and waking up to take care of a crying baby," Adler said, staring at the floor.

Dennis wanted to tell Adler how lucky he was. He had a family while Dennis had nobody. He went to bed alone, and even his parents had rejected him. He did not want to admit it to Adler, but sometimes he felt so lonely. Being a Marine and having a boyfriend did not fit in the same sentence, and Dennis did not want to take a girlfriend who would be just an act. At least he had that much self-respect left.

"You'll be a great dad," Dennis said.

"I don't know," Adler said before pausing. Then he drained the last of his coffee and said, "Let's go see check how Newton feels."

They walked to the medical center and found Newton reading a book on his bed. The color had returned on his face, and he smiled as soon as he saw Dennis and Adler.

"I didn't know you could read." Dennis smirked.

"Asshole," Newton said, still smiling.

"Feeling better?" Adler asked.

"Yes, sir," Newton said. "It was just some virus. They need to run a couple of tests today. If everything's okay, they'll let me go," he added.

The door to the patient room opened, and Jafar stepped in. He saw Dennis and stopped, but then quickly gave him a weak smile before he walked to Newton's bed. He took a stethoscope and asked Newton to open his shirt so that he could listen to his lungs.

"How do they sound?" Newton asked.

"I'm not sure," Jafar said and moved the scope a bit. "I've never done this before. I don't know how they should sound," he added, embarrassed.

"They didn't teach that in nursing school?" Dennis said, surprised.

Jafar shook his head and blushed. The Marines looked at him and waited to see what he would do next. Jafar felt uncomfortable. *How am I supposed to be in charge here when I can't even manage a simple procedure?*

"You can test mine and then compare it to his," Dennis said, taking off his shirt.

"I didn't know you could think," Newton said to Dennis.

Jafar approached Dennis and put the scope on his chest. He was nervous, and his hands were shaking a bit when he moved the stethoscope to different places.

Dennis felt Jafar's hands on his chest and hoped that the other Marines would not notice the swelling in his pants. Casually, he put his left hand in his pocket.

"I think you are okay. You both sound the same," Jafar said softly after he had listened to both of them a couple of times.

"If I sound like him, I'm definitely sick," Newton said.

Jafar laughed. "I'll still check your temperature."

"Let's see," Dennis said and put his hand on Newton's forehead. "He's not hot," he said.

"And you think you are?" Newton said.

"Hotter than you, ugly boy," Dennis said.

Newton did not have a fever so, after calling Doctor Lienert, Jafar told Newton he could leave the hospital. Newton dressed in his uniform, and the three Marines left together.

Jafar took the linens from Newton's bed and put them in the washing machine before he started to clean the patient room. Thoughts of Dennis were storming in his head. Being close to Dennis and touching his muscular chest shouldn't have felt so good. It was wrong, but he couldn't stop thinking of him.

Over the next couple of days, Dennis saw hardly a glimpse of Jafar. It was like the nurse was avoiding him on purpose. On Saturday morning, Dennis finally got his chance to talk with Jafar. He had woken up earlier than usual. When he arrived in the cafeteria for breakfast, he saw Jafar sitting alone, unable to escape him this time.

"Do you mind if I sit here?" Dennis said, sitting before Jafar could answer.

"Hi, Dennis." Jafar smiled shyly.

"Look, I'm sorry for what I said the other day," Dennis said.

"It's okay."

"I was wondering if we could eat dinner today in town," Dennis said hesitantly. "Not in the same place, and I understand if you don't want to," he added quickly.

"That would be nice," Jafar said cheerfully.

Dennis could not help smiling. He was watching the cute, small guy as he finished his breakfast. Jafar's skin was dark brown, and his hair was even darker, almost black. It was rather short but not curly like many Africans had. His eyes were brown, too, and brightened by his friendly smile.

They walked to the yard together and stopped before they had to separate. Dennis' gaze lingered on the attractive nurse whom he would soon take on a date. Technically speaking, it was not a date, but Dennis wanted to think it was. Jafar was smiling at him, and Dennis hoped he thought of the dinner in the same way. Finally, Jafar left for the medical center, and Dennis went to his room where he found Adler and Newton. They chatted and played some cards, but most of the day, Dennis was thinking of Jafar.

When the sun was setting, Dennis and Jafar walked to the parking area and hopped into Jafar's car. They drove east to a restaurant called Queen of Sheba. Dennis had read on the Internet that it was one of the best restaurants in Juba. The prices in South Sudan were cheap, even for an American Marine, and Dennis had no problem paying for both of them.

The restaurant was half-full of customers, and peaceful music was playing in the background. A young waiter guided them to a table and lit the candle. It felt rather romantic to Dennis, who hoped that Jafar would not feel uncomfortable. At least he seemed to be okay.

"I'll let you choose," Dennis said, and closed his menu.

"What would you like?" Jafar said.

"Something local." Dennis looked Jafar deep in his beautiful eyes. Jafar smiled shyly at him.

Jafar gave their order, and the waiter soon returned with a jug of water. He was carrying a glass of wine for Dennis in his other hand. Dennis would have preferred beer, but the waiter had convinced him that wine would fit better with the fish. Maybe he was right; Dennis was not particularly a wine expert. When he went out with his teammates, he always chose to drink beer. In a gay club, he could order sweet cocktails, something that he was too embarrassed to do in front of the other Marines.

It did not take long for the waiter to bring their starters. Dennis looked at his plate and saw some green salad and vegetables he did not recognize. And then there was the fish, the reason he could not drink beer.

"This is good," Dennis said after he had tasted the fish.

"It's tilapia from the River Nile," Jafar said, "steamed with lime."

"Hmm … normally, if I have to eat fish, it's salmon or tuna."

"You don't like fish?" Jafar asked, worried.

"I'm a meat-eater," Dennis said. "Oh. Don't get me wrong. This is delicious. Maybe you could teach me to eat more fish."

"I can do that," Jafar said softly and smiled.

Once they had finished, the waiter took their plates and brought the main course. To Dennis' disappointment, it was vegetarian. It looked like a pita bread filled with onion, tomatoes, and beans. Dennis did not say anything because he did not want to hurt Jafar's feelings. Bravely, he picked up the fork and knife and started to eat.

"Oh my god. This is so good," Dennis said.

"Says the carnivore," Jafar said.

"Screw you. But you are really expanding my horizons," Dennis said.

Jafar was pleased that his American guest enjoyed the Sudanese cuisine and the food that he had chosen from the menu. He found Dennis funny and easy-going and liked spending time with him. He did not know how long the Marines would be there to protect the embassy, but he was painfully aware that his own time at the embassy would soon come to an end.

"Soon I'll become a farmer," Jafar said, trying to hide the disappointment in his voice.

"A farmer? Why?" Dennis asked.

"When I marry Amira, my cousin, I'll move to her parents' house," Jafar explained. "I'll be helping my father-in-law with the farm work."

"So, you'll stop working at the embassy?" Dennis' disappointment was plain in his voice.

"That's the plan," Jafar said.

Dennis had no idea how long their assignment at the embassy would last, but he had had high hopes of spending some intimate moments with the good-looking nurse. Jafar was a couple of years younger, and his boyish look appealed to Dennis. Now it seemed that he had to forget that idea.

They finished their vegetarian dishes, Dennis paid the bill, and then they left the restaurant. It had rained a bit, and the headlights of Jafar's Toyota reflected from the wet asphalt when they drove back to the embassy. The sun had set hours ago, and it was dark.

Dennis was alert and kept watching for possible threats. He knew that they should have returned to the embassy earlier. The resistance was moving toward the center of Juba, where the government buildings and the US Embassy were, and they had heard several gunshots every night. Dennis had deliberately failed to inform the Chief of Staff about this trip. He hoped the self-important officer would have already noticed that he was gone. That would make him pace around his office and blow off steam like a locomotive.

They had to change their route twice to avoid bigger crowds, but they made it safe to the embassy. Dennis felt sorry for Jafar, who had to live his entire life in a place like this. Maybe he was used to this and did not know of a better life.

Jafar went to the medical center to see if anyone needed his help, and Dennis walked to the side entrance of the main building. He used his key card to open the metal door and climbed the stairs to the second door.

"It's my turn," Dennis said, and knocked on the door of the guardroom. Private Newton opened the door.

"You're early," Newton said.

"I don't mind." Dennis shrugged. "You can go sleep. I'll watch some porn here and jerk off."

"Tell me something I don't know." Newton smirked and left.

Dennis walked to the window, which was bullet-proof and provided a good view of the main gate. A high brick wall surrounded the embassy, and they had closed all other gates, which meant that the main gate, illuminated by bright spotlights, was the only entrance to the embassy. The yard was empty, and Dennis could see two armed guards at the gate.

The Marines monitored the embassy from the guardroom twenty-four/seven using six-hour turns. It was a rather easy job. Sixteen surveillance cameras broadcasted live stream to the monitors, and forty-five motion sensors gave a warning signal if somebody was moving in the embassy buildings.

Dennis had sat on the sofa and watched television for twenty minutes when the control panel gave a warning signal. He assumed that one of the Marines had gone to the bathroom, but he decided to check the monitor. The residence building was black on the screen; there had been no movement after Newton had gone to his room. The warning signal had come from the staircase that led to the guardroom.

"What the fuck?" Dennis muttered.

Dennis started to rewind the recording from the camera that was outside the side entrance. He did not have time to see anybody in the recording before he heard a knock on the door.

"Who's there?" Dennis said, sliding quickly so that he was leaning against the wall on the right side of the door. He knew that most people tried to shoot through the door.

"It's me," Dennis heard Jafar whispering.

Smiling, Dennis let Jafar in and locked the door again. He was not sure if he was allowed to let outsiders into the guardroom, but he enjoyed Jafar's company, so he decided not to worry too much. Besides, it was night, so nobody would find out.

"I hope you don't mind…," Jafar said, like he did not even know himself why he had come to see Dennis.

"Not at all. It's nice to have some company," Dennis said.

"Good," Jafar said, clearly relaxing. "I brought some candies," he said, smiling as he took a big candy pouch from his pocket.

They sat on the sofa, and Jafar put the candy pouch between them. Every now and then, when Jafar took candies from the pouch, Dennis put his hand on the pouch simultaneously, on purpose, so that their hands touched each other. Jafar's hand felt soft against his skin, which aroused him.

"You know what I dream of when I go to bed?" Jafar said, looking away from Dennis.

I wish you dreamed of me, Dennis thought, but said nothing.

"I dream of moving to America," Jafar said, still staring at the opposite wall.

"Oh," Dennis said.

"That's why I applied for a job here at the embassy."

The monitor beeped again, and Dennis checked the security cameras only to notice that Adler had gone to the bathroom. He returned to the sofa and sat closer to Jafar so that their legs were almost touching. Jafar did not move away; maybe he did not even realize that Dennis had gotten closer.

"How about being a farmer? Is that part of your dream?" Dennis asked.

The silence stretched before Jafar admitted, "Not really."

"So, why don't you follow your dream then?"

"My father has decided on a different path for me," Jafar said, and looked at Dennis.

Dennis saw sadness in Jafar's beautiful eyes. It was the same sadness he felt during the lonely nights when he missed somebody in his bed, not just for sex, but to hold close and love. It was his dream—a dream that his parents did not want for him, and something that his military career made difficult to come true.

"What do you dream of?" Jafar asked, as if he were reading Dennis' mind.

"Um … I would like to be happy," Dennis said.

Under normal circumstances, Dennis would have joked or said something sarcastic, but there was something in Jafar that forced him to answer seriously. He was not used to it, and it made him feel uncomfortable.

"And what would make you happy?" Jafar said.

"What would make me happy...?" Dennis repeated and took a better position on the sofa. "A relationship. Someone to love," he said finally.

"That's what I like about America. You can choose to do things that make you happy."

"Yeah, that's great," Dennis said. *I wish it were that easy.*

They sat for a while in silence and watched the TV. Occasionally they heard some distant gunshots. Luckily, the blocks around the embassy were peaceful. The government offices were empty, and those few people who lived in the neighborhood were sleeping, either on their beds or in the nearby park.

When the TV program ended, Dennis rose and turned off the TV. He switched off the lights and walked to the big window with the nice view of the sleeping city. Jafar joined him, and they stood there shoulder by shoulder, watching out.

"I'm gonna miss this place," Jafar said.

"I wish you could follow your dream," Dennis said and put his arm on Jafar's shoulder.

"Me, too." Jafar turned to look at Dennis.

They stared at each other, and for a moment, Dennis hoped that they would kiss. Then the security monitor gave a signal, and Dennis had to check what had triggered the alarm. The first alarm came from the residence building, soon followed by another from the staircase behind the guardroom door. It was Adler.

"I couldn't sleep, so I decided to take my shift and let you go to bed," Adler said when Dennis opened the door for him.

"How thoughtful of you," Dennis said, slightly irritated that Adler had interrupted them.

"I guess you had enough time to jerk—" Adler said, stopping abruptly when he saw Jafar in the dim room. "Oh, you have company."

"Yeah, we were watching TV," Dennis said.

"Um … I think I should leave now." Before either Marine could respond, Jafar left the room.

Dennis gave Adler a quick report and walked down the stairs to the yard. Jafar was nowhere to be seen, so Dennis went straight to bed. Soon, the sound of his loud snoring filled the room.

The following morning, Adler rushed into the room, waking Dennis who realized immediately that something was going on. He rose to sit on the bed, covering his erection with the white blanket.

"What's going on?" he asked, yawning.

"Come on! We need to go to the operations room. Headquarters calling," Adler said.

"Maybe we're going back home," Dennis said, sounding hopeful.

"Maybe," Adler said, "or maybe not."

Chapter 6

Dennis grabbed a cup of coffee from the cafeteria, ignoring Adler who constantly asked him to hurry, and they walked to the operations room, which was on the ground floor of the main building. The room was windowless and dark, and the only light came from the dimmed spotlights on the ceiling. Ambassador Witt and his Chief of Staff were sitting there with Newton and Mullen.

"Finally," the Chief of Staff muttered when Dennis and Adler sat down.

"Sorry, I had to change into my uniform," Dennis smirked at the Chief of Staff.

"Mark, could you please open the connection?" the ambassador asked jovially.

The Chief of Staff pressed a couple of buttons on the remote control that was attached to the table, and the big screen on the wall went off. He cursed a couple of times and browsed the menus for a while before he found out how to open the line. Finally, they saw a man staring at them on the screen.

"I'm Captain Mills from the Marine Corps Special Operations Center, and I am here with Major General Christensen," the man said, and turned the camera a bit so that they could see General Christensen.

"Good morning, gentlemen, or whatever time it is there," General Christensen said wryly. "I'm the Commander of MARSOC, as you should know."

"Good morning," the ambassador said. "I'm Ambassador Witt, as you should also know." He flashed a smile.

"First of all, I want the ambassador and the other civilian to leave the room. This is military business," General Christensen said.

"This is my embassy. I want to know what is going on in here," the ambassador protested.

"As I said, this is military business, and I appreciate your cooperation," the general replied.

The ambassador and the Chief of Staff looked at each other, obviously dissatisfied that they were asked to leave the room. Dennis was smiling at the Chief of Staff, which increased his irritation. Finally, the ambassador stood up and walked out of the door, followed by the Chief of Staff, who slammed the door.

"Welcome to Operation Silent Moon," General Christensen said. "I'm sure you have been wondering why we sent you there."

"You sent us? I thought it was the embassy security group," Adler said.

"You were sent by Special Operations Command," General Christensen said after a short pause. "The big boys in Tampa," he added and snorted.

"And what is our mission, sir?" Adler asked.

"Captain Mills will tell you that shortly," General Christensen said, "but I want you to understand that this is top secret. This mission comes from the White House, which we will obviously deny should anything happen to you."

The Marines looked at each other. The whole time Dennis had had the feeling that something was wrong. They would never send a force recon team to protect an embassy, and the evacuation had felt a rather strong measure considering that the district of Hai-Amarat was relatively peaceful and the other embassies and government buildings were fully operational.

"The evacuation … it's part of the operation?" Dennis said.

"That's correct, Corporal Benson. We want as few people to witness this operation as possible," Captain Mills said.

"We sent you there to assassinate Shaker Salih, Chief Administrator of the Sudan People's Liberation Movement," General Christensen interrupted.

"Why all this secrecy, sir, if we're just going to kill one guy?" Adler said.

"Sergeant Williams, the situation in South Sudan is challenging. You might have noticed that there is a civil war going on. Many have their own interests there, including the White House," General Christensen said.

"The United Nations daydreams that they are in control. The African Union has a lot of troops there, mostly Ethiopians. And the Europeans want to use diplomatic channels to solve the conflict," Captain Mills said.

"So, you understand how the rest of the world would react if they knew that Uncle Sam solved this conflict for them," General Christensen said.

Captain Mills explained the details of their mission. After sunset, they would be taken in a military helicopter near Abyei Town, which was located on the border between the Republic of Sudan and South Sudan. Their latest intel on Shaker Salih's whereabouts pointed there.

Abyei Town was the capital of the Abyei Area, which was accorded special administrative status in the peace agreement that ended the twenty-two-year-long Second Sudanese Civil War. South Sudan had claimed the area, but it was currently controlled by the northern Sudanese government. The residents of the area were, on an interim basis, citizens of both South Sudan and the Republic of Sudan.

"Once your mission is completed, you will be transported to Kenya, and from there you will fly immediately back to Camp Pendleton," Captain Mills said. "During the mission, you will communicate only with me."

"Nobody knows where you are. And you can't return to Juba. Understood?" General Christensen said.

"Yes, sir," Adler said.

"Sir, how about the ambassador and the Chief of Staff?" Dennis asked.

"You will tell them nothing. We'll take care of the rest," General Christensen said.

Dennis thought that the mission would be relatively easy, even though it seemed to be highly important. According to the satellite images that Captain Mills had showed them, Abyei Town was a small town and badly damaged by the war. The infrastructure there was not advanced enough that the locals could have built bunkers or other hiding places. They were professionals; eliminating some villain should be a piece of cake.

"There is an encrypted fax line in your room. I'll send you some maps and other documents," Captain Mills said.

"Okay, sir," Adler said as he rose from his seat to fetch the papers.

"Good luck, boys. Come home alive," General Christensen said. Then the video connection was closed.

"Last day here. Let's go prepare," Adler said to the other Marines.

"Finally some action," Newton said, excited.

They left the operations room and walked the narrow stairs up to a small lobby in the administration wing. They saw the Chief of Staff in his office. He glared at them but lowered his gaze quickly back to his papers.

"So, your meeting is finished," the Chief of Staff shouted.

"Yes, it is," Dennis said, knowing that the Chief of Staff would have wanted some details.

Dennis enjoyed the situation. He did not like the snooty Chief of Staff, and it gave him a lot of satisfaction to play with the man. He had no intention of revealing anything to him.

"It was an interesting meeting," he shouted. "Unfortunately, military business," he added, and zipped his lips with his fingers.

"You're evil," Adler said.

"My middle name." Dennis grinned.

They had packed everything by lunchtime, and after a quick lunch, they stayed in the empty cafeteria and talked about the mission. They were all excited that they would finally see some action, but they all understood that it was a risky mission. If something went wrong, they were on their own. Special Operations Command could not send reinforcements to support them since the operation was not authorized by the UN or the African Union.

"I'll take my last turn in the guardroom," Adler said as they were finishing their meeting. "Besides, the security guard has been there for a long time already."

"They have to get used to it when we are gone," Newton said, "but I really admire your work ethic."

"Work ethic, my ass," Dennis said. "He just wants some privacy to jerk off."

"Screw you," Adler said, smiling as he walked away.

Dennis decided to take a nap and started to walk toward the residence building. In the second floor corridor, he saw Jafar, who looked sad and lost.

"Something wrong?" Dennis said.

"I just resigned," Jafar said in a small voice. "Next week is my last week here."

Today is my last day here, Dennis thought, but he knew that he could not tell Jafar that.

"Come in," Dennis said, and opened the door to his room.

They sat on the bed, and Jafar was so small and miserable that Dennis wanted to hug him. Finally, he could not resist the urge and wrapped his arms around the shaking boy. Jafar did not resist, but he sobbed silently against his muscular chest. Dennis felt the electricity in his body as he held the cute nurse so close to him.

Today is my last day here, Dennis thought again, and let his arms wander a bit over Jafar's body. Jafar did not push Dennis away but moved even a bit closer to him. Dennis could hear how Jafar was breathing lightly.

Dennis felt his penis starting to swell, making quite a noticeable bulge in his camo pants. He was worried that it would make Jafar uneasy, and he tried to will it down, but lost the battle; it just kept growing. In no time, he was hard as a rock.

"What's wrong with me?" Jafar asked in a voice that was barely audible.

"What do you mean?" Dennis said, still holding the boy.

"I can't stop thinking of you," Jafar said. "And this … this makes me feel good…. It makes me … you know," he said, embarrassed.

Dennis moved his hand slowly toward Jafar's crotch, stopping every now and then to check his reaction. Since Jafar did not stop him, he took lightly hold of Jafar's erection through his pants. It throbbed in his hand.

"You mean I make you hard?" Dennis said softly.

"Yes," Jafar whispered.

"You make me hard, too," Dennis said and guided Jafar's hand to his erection.

"But this is wrong," Jafar said, unable to pull his hand away.

"Why do you think so?" Dennis asked, rubbing Jafar's erection softly.

"They would kill me if they knew," Jafar said, and started crying.

It was like all the pain in the world smashed the small boy. Dennis held him on his lap, occasionally petting his hair, and Jafar cried until there were no more tears left. Then he turned and looked at Dennis with his red eyes.

"Is it okay to … feel this way in America?" he said.

"Sure," Dennis said. *Except if you are a Marine or have conservative bigots as parents*, he thought bitterly.

"Then I want to move to America," Jafar said wistfully.

Yeah, but you will soon move to a farm and marry a fourteen-year-old girl, Dennis thought, but said nothing. Life often seemed to be unfair. This kind and sweet kid did not deserve such a destiny.

Dennis lay down on the bed and pulled Jafar gently on top of him. Jafar felt light on top of his muscular body. He wrapped his arms around Jafar and hugged him tenderly. He was surprised when Jafar suddenly kissed him.

"I have never felt anything like this," Jafar said honestly.

Me neither, Dennis thought, but was too afraid to say it aloud. He realized that he was developing feelings for Jafar, and it was something that had never happened before. All the guys he had been with before had just been the result of his search for a quick relief. Jafar was something else.

They kissed again. And again. And then, suddenly, the door opened and Adler stepped in. Jafar, who was lying on top of Dennis, freaked out. Quickly he backed up to the farthest corner and stared at Adler in fright.

"Oh … sorry, I should have knocked," Adler said, confused.

"Um," Dennis said, and rubbed his hands nervously.

"I think I should go," Adler said hesitantly and left the room, closing the door behind him.

Dennis looked at Jafar, who was shaking in the corner. He tried to move closer, but Jafar raised his hand to stop him.

"He will tell my father!" Jafar said in panic.

"No, he won't," Dennis said, trying to calm him down.

"How can you be so sure?" Jafar said bluntly. "I'm dead if he does," he said, raising his voice.

"First, he doesn't know your father. And second, we're leaving tonight to go to Abyei Town, and we'll never come back," Dennis said, raising his voice, too.

As soon as he had said it, he regretted it. He should not have revealed any detail of their secret mission to Jafar. And what was even worse, telling him now that they would never meet again made Dennis feel like some molester who had just tried to take advantage of Jafar and then leave. That had never been his intention.

"Oh…," Jafar said. Dennis was not sure if he was angry, confused, or even relieved.

"Look, they told us this morning that we will leave today," Dennis said, "and I'm sorry for what just happened. I did not mean to come on to you."

"Don't be sorry. I liked it," Jafar said, smiling sadly. "I liked it a lot."

They hugged for a long time. Then Dennis took a picture of him from his bag and gave it to Jafar. Adler had taken the picture in front of the embassy and printed it in the office since he thought Dennis looked funny. He had attached it to their door to entertain Newton and Mullen. Dennis had been quicker and hid the picture in his bag.

"You look cute," Jafar said shyly, looking at the picture.

"Your ass is cute," Dennis said.

They hugged again and said goodbye to each other, knowing they would never meet again. No matter how tough Marine Dennis thought he was, there were still tears in his eyes when he watched Jafar walking away.

Chapter 7

Dennis hurried down a long corridor into the bunker, which was under the embassy main building. Adler had caught him and Jafar in the act a couple of hours earlier, and Dennis had not had a chance to talk with Adler privately. Actually, he had not even seen Adler before he stepped into the bunker and saw his teammates changing into their combat uniforms.

"Great, Corporal Benson decided to join the mission," Adler said nonchalantly. He was wearing only his boxers.

"Huh? Yeah, I thought I should join the party," Dennis said. Not knowing what Adler was thinking of him made him nervous.

"Okay then, get changed," Adler said and dropped his boxers to change them to clean ones.

"Yes, sir," Dennis said, and took his combat utility uniform from his bag.

In seven minutes, the team was ready. They climbed the stairs to the roof to wait for the helicopter. Soon, the massive rumble of the engines of the UH-1Y Venom military helicopter, or Yankee as they called it, filled the air. The Marines stepped in, and the helicopter left immediately. The sun had set, bathing the city in darkness.

Dennis sat close to Adler in the small cabin; their legs and shoulders were touching. Adler had seen him making out with another man, but now he did not give the slightest hint what he thought about it. Dennis would have wanted to explain it somehow, but the only way to communicate inside the helicopter was to use the mic and the headphones, and he did not want to have the discussion while Newton and Mullen were listening.

"Nervous, Benson? You're surprisingly quiet," Newton said into his microphone.

"Huh? Just thinking," Dennis said. Adler looked at him and nodded.

"He's just sad because he lost his chance with the hot chick in the cafeteria," Mulled said.

"Something like that," Dennis said.

Apparently Adler had not told Newton and Mullen what he had seen a couple of hours earlier. Dennis assumed that was a good sign. He had to talk with Adler, but it could take several days before their mission was over and they would have an opportunity to talk. That bothered him, but there was nothing he could do about it right now, so he forced his focus on the mission at hand.

I wish I could've spent a couple of days more with him. Dennis thought of Jafar and saw how the lights of Juba became smaller and smaller when the Yankee ascended to the sky. He felt sad, and he had to swallow a couple of times to gain control of his emotions. *Fuck, I'm trained to handle these things. I should just forget him*, he thought but could not get Jafar out of his mind.

The engines grumbled, and every now and then, the pilot changed the course a bit on their way north. Dennis looked out of the window but could see only darkness everywhere. The pilot was clearly avoiding flying near big cities.

"We'll reach our destination in ten minutes," the pilot said over the intercom after they had been flying almost two hours.

"Get ready to climb down," Adler said.

Dennis checked that his equipment was in place and dropped his flashlight in the process. He tried to catch it, but it rolled under the seat. He made a mental note to grab it before they left the helicopter.

"This is US Special Operations Command. Abort the mission!" the operator at MacDill Air Force Base in Tampa said urgently on the phone.

"Marine Special Operations Command requests confirmation to abort Silent Moon," Captain Mills replied from Camp Pendleton as he rose from his seat.

"Confirmed, MARSOC. Abort the mission," the USSOCOM operator said.

"Night Fox, abort Silent Moon," Captain Mills said into his microphone. "Fly to direction 195 and wait for more information," he added.

The line was silent. There was no reply from the team in South Sudan.

"Night Fox, this is MARSOC. Do you copy? Abort Silent Moon," Captain Mills said. It was not the first mission he had led, but there was some nervousness in his voice.

Still no reply from South Sudan.

"Are they still visible on the radar?" General Christensen said.

"No, sir," the Marine in front of the control table said.

"What the hell is going on? And why does USSOCOM want to abort the mission?" General Christensen said angrily.

"Sir, General Boyd from USSOCOM wants to talk to us," the MARSOC operator shouted.

"Open the line," General Christensen said.

The operators in MacDill Air Force Base and Camp Pendleton Marine Base opened a secured video connection between the operations rooms at both bases. Soon the face of General Boyd appeared on the screen.

"I'm General Boyd, and I'm the Commander of USSOCOM," General Boyd said.

"Sir, could you please explain what is going on?" General Christensen said.

Technically speaking, they were both generals, but when it came to Special Operations, General Boyd was General Christensen's boss, which was a source of irritation Christensen chose to ignore for the moment. The priority was to get on top of the situation.

"Three minutes ago, we received intel saying that the Sudan People's Liberation Movement is equipped with heavy anti-aircraft missiles," General Boyd said.

"What? Where the fuck did they get those?" General Christensen said.

"We don't know yet, but it seems they were expecting us," General Boyd said.

"Were they shot down?" Captain Mills asked.

"Sir, the automatic emergency module of the helicopter reported a crash and a heavy explosion soon before it went dead," one of the Marines in Camp Pendleton read from his screen.

"Fuck," General Boyd said. "Clear the room. Christensen and Mills, stay," he ordered.

The Marines at the MARSOC operations room in Camp Pendleton left the room quickly. General Christensen and Captain Mills took seats in front of the big video screen. The mission had failed, and they had potentially a big mess to clean.

"We cannot send more troops there," General Boyd said. "The UN and the African Union cannot get any information about the mission."

"But what if the team is still alive? And what if the Liberation Movement finds the helicopter?" Captain Mills asked, surprised.

"It's highly unlikely that they would survive an explosion that destroyed the entire emergency module of a Yankee helicopter," General Christensen said.

"Why do you think so?" General Boyd said.

"It's heavily replicated. There are three independent transmitters, which are now all dead," General Christensen said, looking at the report that one of the Marines had left him.

General Boyd looked suddenly satisfied. He tried to hide his smile; after all, they had just lost four Marines.

"So, we have reason to believe that there are no survivors and the explosion destroyed all possible evidence," General Boyd said.

"I would say so, sir," General Christensen said, realizing where this discussion was going.

"Then we have no reason for a rescue mission," General Boyd said. "Besides, if the Liberation Movements shoots down a military helicopter, they are not likely to report it to anybody."

"That's correct, sir," General Christensen said, relaxing. "I'll ask the Reconnaissance Battalion to inform the families of the deceased."

Captain Mills wanted to disagree, but he decided it was useless. Two superior officers had decided how to clean up this mess. The only thing he could do was to follow the standard procedure: go to a bar, drink as much as was required to forget his lost colleagues, and move on with his own life.

"Just one more thing," General Boyd said, "do you think the ambassador or the other embassy staff form a security risk?"

"I don't think they do," General Christensen said after thinking awhile. "Most of the embassy staff was evacuated, and Ambassador Witt isn't aware of the mission," he reasoned.

If General Boyd was dissatisfied with the answer, he did not say anything. Captain Mills noted, though, that the smile had disappeared from his face. Even if the embassy staff had been a security risk, Mills did not understand what the generals could do to keep them silent.

The next morning, Jafar woke up to someone knocking at his door. He was tired since he had been thinking most of the night of Dennis and what had happened in his room. The memory was sweet except for the ending where Adler walked into the room and Dennis left Juba for good.

Jafar opened the door and was frightened when he saw Ambassador Witt standing in the corridor. His face was severe. *He knows, and they're coming to get me*, Jafar thought and instinctively took a couple of steps back.

"Jafar, good that you are here," the ambassador said. "Please prepare the medical center for emergency."

"Why? What has happened?" Jafar asked, worried.

"We received a call last night for mayday from a helicopter pilot near Abyei Town. We are the closest embassy, and they may need our help today."

"Oh my god," Jafar said, and went pale. "Is it the group of Marines who left from here to Abyei yesterday?"

"They left to Abyei?" the ambassador said, surprised. "They told me they were returning to California."

Obviously the ambassador was not aware of the military operation that was going on, which surprised Jafar. Then he remembered how Dennis had emphasized how important it was that he did not tell anybody anything about the operation, which he had heard of by accident. It seemed that the ambassador was also an "anybody" in that respect.

"Have we heard anything since the call for mayday?" Jafar asked.

"Nothing. I even contacted the State Department, and they said that we didn't have any helicopters flying in Abyei last night," the ambassador said. "Maybe I should contact Special Operations Command and check if it really was those Marines."

"That sound like a good idea," Jafar said. He was worried and wanted to know what had happened to Dennis, if it was their helicopter.

"Let's be prepared to use the cold room in the kitchen. Since we have not heard anything for hours, I don't expect them to bring more than bodies here," the ambassador said and left.

Jafar knew that the ambassador was right. The nights in Abyei were cold; at this time of year, the temperature dropped close to freezing. On the other hand, it was blazing hot in the afternoon. If there had been an accident and they were still alive, they would not be long—especially if they were severely injured. He hoped the ambassador was able to find out what had happened.

For the first time during his assignment in Juba, the ambassador was furious. He stormed to his room, picked up the phone, and asked the operator to connect him to General Boyd. He had no idea what the local time was at Special Operations Command in Tampa, and he did not even care.

In the meanwhile, Jafar went to the cafeteria to get some breakfast. He was not especially hungry but forced himself to eat some eggs and bacon, yet another thing that would have made his father furious. According to the Quran, the consumption of pork was strictly forbidden. In his paradise, Jafar had his own rules.

After breakfast, Jafar left the cafeteria and walked toward the medical center. He was in the yard, a couple of steps from the medical center front door, when he heard a loud explosion behind him. The windows of the main building were broken, and Jafar saw fire everywhere. He stood in shock, unable to move, and watched as a big part of the roof collapsed.

The guard at the gate was lying on the ground, and his face was covered in blood. Jafar ran to help him but realized that the guard was dead. Jafar could not find a pulse from his neck but saw how a bullet had pierced his forehead near his left eye. He felt sick and had to turn his head away.

After recovering from the dead guard, Jafar realized that somebody was moving on the roof of the medical center. He was about to shout for help when the person on the roof opened fire toward the residence building. A couple of embassy employees had still been inside, and they had rushed out when they heard the explosion. They were now lying dead on the yard in front of the building. Jafar moved quietly close to the medical center wall, hoping that the person on the roof could not see him there.

The gate was closed, and the only guard on duty had been killed. That meant that Jafar could not escape through the gate. He waited a while and sneaked inside through the medical center door. Scared that they would soon blow up the medical center, he ran along the corridor to the last patient room on the right. When he entered the room, he heard a new explosion and assumed it was the residence building. He had to hurry if he wanted to escape the embassy alive.

Jafar remembered there was a window to the street in the patient room. Unfortunately, he had forgotten that the window had strong steel bars. Desperately, he took hold of the bars and pulled as hard as he could. They did not budge.

Jafar ran to the supply room. If he was lucky, he could find a screwdriver that he could use to remove the bars. He scanned the shelves and opened every box he could find. Finally, he found a set of screwdrivers. He took them, rushed back to the patient room, and started to loosen the screws.

It felt like removing the bars would take forever. He used all his strength to loosen the screws, which were tightened fast. Once he had removed half of them, he was sweaty and tired, and he had to rest for a while. The pause was short since he heard some noise from the lobby. As quietly as possible, he locked the patient room door and continued removing the screws.

He was loosening the last screw when someone tried to open the patient room. Jafar's heart stopped. The handle was turned again, but the door did not open. Jafar held his breath and heard steps moving away from the door. Unable to wait longer, Jafar took a chair and threw it through the window. The glass broke into thousands of pieces and made a horrible noise.

Jafar climbed out of the window and, without looking back, ran to his car as fast as he could. The wounds in his arms and legs, which he had got from the broken glass, were bleeding. He did not care. The only thing that mattered was to stay alive.

The next problem waited when he got to his car. All the wheels had been cut with something sharp, and the windshield was broken. Jafar looked around but could not see anybody. Silently, he opened the right back door and lay down on the backseat, closing the door. He hoped that whoever had tried to kill him would not come to look for him there.

After waiting at least an hour, he finally came out of the car. The car was hot as hell, and he had to drink something. Also, the street was full of police officers and firemen trying to get the situation in the embassy under control, so he assumed that, even if the killer or killers were waiting for him, he could hide in the crowd of people.

He ran six blocks until he got to the Muniki roundabout and called his brother. He explained what had happened, and fifteen long minutes later, he saw Abdul's car. Only when Abdul dropped him at their house did he believe that he had survived.

"What happened?" Jafar's mother asked.

"The embassy was attacked. I think everybody else is dead," Jafar said. "And they tried to kill me too," he added, still in shock.

"You should thank Allah that he saved you," his mother said calmly.

"I will," Jafar said hesitantly. He was annoyed that, even thought he had almost died, his mother was more interested in keeping God satisfied.

"And you must talk with your father when he comes home."

"I guess so," Jafar muttered and went to the bedroom that he shared with his younger brother.

Jafar lay down on his bed. He took the picture of Dennis from his pocket, feeling happiness when he looked at Dennis' handsome face and muscular chest. He was satisfied that he had taken the picture with him that morning and had not left it in his room in the embassy. Then he realized that Dennis must have died in the accident in Abyei last night, and it made him suddenly miserable.

Tears were running down his cheeks as he stared at the smiling boy in the picture and thought about his move to the farm in the countryside next weekend. *I'll spend the rest of my life there as a slave to my father-in-law*, he thought and hid the picture under his mattress.

Chapter 8

The twin-engine Yankee utility helicopter banked right, and then the pilot prepared to land. They had approached the place where the Marines would leave the helicopter and start their mission. Dennis looked at his teammates and felt the excitement in the air. Newton's smile was self-assured, but it was most likely just to cover his nervousness.

Suddenly the pilot pulled up. The helicopter jerked heavily so that Dennis had to take hold of Adler's leg. The Marines turned to look at the pilot, trying to understand what had happened. Then they heard an explosion and saw a big fireball. A missile had hit the left engine, soon followed by another missile that destroyed the tail rotor.

"This is Night Fox. We've been hit! We're crashing near Abyei Town. Mayday, mayday!" the pilot shouted on the radio.

"Can someone hear us?" Adler asked. "We don't have support troops here," he added, knowing that it was a secret mission.

"Juba Embassy is listening on that frequency," the pilot grunted, trying desperately to control the helicopter. "They're our only hope."

"We are too far away," Adler said. "And even if they heard, it takes at least ten hours to drive here."

Soon after, the fifty-eight-foot-long Yankee, the most capable utility helicopter on the globe, crashed to the ground. The blades dug furrows into the earth before the main rotor system stopped. The self-sealing mechanism of the fuel tanks had failed, and there was a smell of fuel everywhere.

It took a moment for Dennis to understand what had happened. The cockpit was burning, and in the flickering light of the flame, he saw Adler unconscious next to him. His uniform was wet from the leaking fuel.

Without losing a second, Dennis opened the safety belts and pulled Adler from the cabin. He could not see much in the darkness as he pulled Adler thirty feet on the ground and returned to the helicopter.

"Holy shit!" he cried when he saw that both Newton and Mullen were covered with flames.

Dennis tried to get closer to his teammates, but the heat of the burning fuel was unbearable and the flames increased rapidly. He realized that he could do nothing to save them. Worse, the helicopter could explode any minute, leaving Adler alone and unprotected. He returned to his sergeant, who was still lying on the ground unconscious, and started to pull him farther and farther from the helicopter. He had pulled Adler hardly ten feet when the main rotor crashed, cutting the main fuel tank. Dennis felt a massive intake of air.

Instinctively, Dennis threw himself on the ground. Using his body as a cover, Dennis tried to protect Adler from the heavy explosions that kept going on for quite some time before they stopped. Once he thought it was safe, he rose and tried to wake Adler. Most of the flames had died, making it even more difficult for Dennis to see Adler's face. Finally, he heard a weak groan.

"Adler, are you okay?"

"What happened?" Adler asked.

"The helicopter crashed," Dennis said, not sure how much information Adler could digest.

"Where are Newton and Mullen?" Adler asked with some panic in his voice.

"They are dead. I could not save them," Dennis admitted, looking down. "I tried my best, though," he added, mostly to himself.

Adler was about to say something when they heard some noise from the east. Glancing over, they saw the headlights of three or four vehicles driving toward them. For a short moment, Dennis felt relieved that the rescuers were coming so quickly before he realized that it was not a rescue team. The Liberation Movement had shot down the helicopter, and now they were coming to check for survivors.

"We need to leave," Adler said and tried to rise from the ground.

"This way." Dennis pointed west.

"No, we can't go there," Adler said. "They're coming from the east. They'll see us in their headlights."

"North then," Dennis decided, and started moving.

"Ouch! Shit," Adler cried. "I can't walk. My ankle is broken."

"Wait, I'll help," Dennis said, and returned to where Adler was standing on one leg.

Worried about the rapidly approaching vehicles, Dennis slung Adler's arm around his shoulders to support him. They limped in the darkness as fast as they could, trying to avoid the headlights that were getting closer and closer. It was hard since they could not see anything, and they kept stumbling over rocks and other obstacles.

"Fuck. This isn't working. We need to hide somewhere," Adler said, after they had fallen down for the third time.

"Do you have a flashlight? I lost mine," Dennis said.

"Yes, but we can't use it. They'll see," Adler said.

Dennis sighed, looking over the desolate landscape filled with hidden traps. "Let's keep going then," he said. "The farther we get, the better. And maybe we'll find a place to hide."

"Okay, but let's move slower," Adler said, holding his injured forearm.

The area near Abyei Town was mostly savanna. The grass was short, and the occasional manketti trees and umbrella thorn acacias gave hardy any hiding place. They heard the sounds of animals and hoped that they would not walk into anything dangerous. Dennis was holding his combat knife in his right hand, hoping he would not have to use it.

Soon the Liberation Movement vehicles reached the site of the helicopter crash. Those were off-road vehicles, rather old, and Dennis estimated that there were five of them. When the last vehicle reached its destination, the driver turned it around before he killed the engine. The headlights scanned the savanna and, for a short time, they pointed directly toward Dennis and Adler, who threw themselves on the ground.

"Did they see us?" Dennis asked.

"I don't think so," Adler said after a while.

The Liberation Movement had parked the cars so that most of the headlights illuminated what was left of the helicopter. Only the final car faced the savanna. A group of men emerged from the cars and studied the crashed helicopter.

"You pulled me out of the Yankee?" Adler said, trying to see what the men were doing.

"Yeah, but you can thank me later," Dennis said.

"I will," Adler said, "but what I meant is that they might see the marks from you pulling me on the ground."

Dennis did not have time to answer before they heard two dogs barking.

"You think those dogs can smell us and lead them here?" Dennis whispered.

"I don't think they've been trained to do that," Adler calmed him down. "But we need to be quiet; they might hear us."

Dennis nodded and then realized Adler couldn't see him. "Makes sense," he whispered.

"Do you have the GPS?" Adler asked.

When Dennis handed him the GPS, he switched it on, covering the bright screen with his body so that the Liberation Movement guys could not see it. It took forever to get a signal, but finally they were able to see their location on the map.

"There's a small river two hundred yards that way," Adler said, and Dennis could barely make out the shadow of his hand pointing.

"Okay, let's crawl there," Dennis said.

"If we cross the river, the dogs will have a harder time smelling us. Assuming they're hunting dogs."

They moved as low and silently as they could, stopping every now and then to listen. Adler found it easier to crawl, but the pain in his ankle was getting worse and worse, making him worried that there was something seriously wrong.

"You need to help me," Adler said once they came to the riverbank.

"Let's go," Dennis said. He tried to carry Adler on his back the best he could.

"Thanks, man," Adler said.

"You're welcome," Dennis said. "This won't be easy," he added after taking a couple of steps in the muddy river.

The water was not deep, but Dennis sank to his knees in the squishy riverbed while carrying the heavy Marine in his back. He was exhausted when they got to the opposite shore, thankfully without being noticed by the Liberation Movement guys, who were still gathered around the crashed Yankee.

"We are soaked," Adler observed as they sat down to rest. "We should find a place where we can dry our uniforms."

"At least you don't smell like fuel anymore," Dennis said, and smirked even though Adler could not see it.

"It'll be cold tonight. It's not even midnight yet. The sun won't rise for several hours," Adler said.

Dennis realized what Adler meant. The water in the river had been warm, but now the cold air made his wet uniform feel almost freezing. They had to find a hiding place, preferably one where they could set a fire that would keep them warm and safe from animals.

"We are too far away from town," Adler said after studying the GPS for quite some time.

"What do you mean? We were supposed to walk there from where the Yankee crashed," Dennis said, confused.

"No, we crashed at least fifteen miles from the planned destination," Adler said, frowning at the screen. "You can't carry me that far tonight."

"You're probably right," Dennis admitted.

They were still pondering their next move when the Liberation Movement guys started the engines of the cars. Dennis followed the lights of the cars until they were not visible anymore. Then total darkness surrounded them. It was interrupted when Adler switched on his flashlight. He pointed the light to his ankle and cursed.

"It's purple and swollen. And hurts like hell," Adler said.

"Here, let me help," Dennis said, and ripped apart his wet shirt.

Dennis cut a couple of branches from a nearby tree and made a bandage out of them and a piece of his shirt. He made it as tight as possible, ignoring Adler's loud protests. Once he was ready, he pointed Adler's flashlight at the makeshift splint.

"Not perfect, but it will do," Dennis said.

"Thanks, that was … painful."

"Pain is my middle name."

It was evident that Adler needed medical help soon, but they hoped that with the bandage he could last a couple of days. At least it would hold his ankle in place in case some bones were broken. The bigger question was how long it would take for them to get back to the embassy in Juba. Dennis was sure that, due to the nature of their mission, MARSOC would not send a rescue team. They were on their own.

"Let's make a plan," Adler said. "What do we have?"

"Two knives, one flashlight, the GPS," Dennis said, fumbling with his belt until he found his pistol. "I've also got my Glock."

"Any water or food?" Adler asked.

"I have one bottle of water, but I don't think we have any food," Dennis said.

"One bottle of water," Adler repeated. "Do you know what this means?"

"We need to find shade before the sun rises," Dennis said, "and stay there the whole day."

Finding a shadowy hiding place at night was easier said than done. Dennis supported Adler, who could put hardly any pressure on his right leg, and they walked slowly toward Abyei Town. After forty-five minutes, they stopped. The savanna had ended, and a terrain of rocks and small hills stretched before them.

"My leg hurts too bad. I can't keep going," Adler said.

"I wish we had the satellite phone. Newton had it, and…," Dennis said, unable to finish the sentence.

"How fucking difficult it is to find a single shadow?" Adler said, frustrated, and flailed with the flashlight.

"Wait!" Dennis took the flashlight from Adler. "There's a small cave there," he said and pointed toward it with the light.

"Awesome," Adler said sarcastically.

Finally, they had some luck. The cave was not big but, according to the GPS, the mouth was to the north. That meant that the sun would not shine there and the small water bottle could be enough to keep them alive one more day.

Dennis helped Adler to the cave and left to collect some wood for a fire. He also decided to bring some soft grass into the cave to sleep on.

We haven't talked about what happened in the embassy, and now we're building a nest, Dennis thought as he pulled the grass from the ground. So far, Adler had not said a word. Maybe he did not want to talk about it. Or maybe he was just in shock after losing two teammates.

Struggling with his thoughts, Dennis gathered a huge pile of grass and turned toward the cave. Then he heard a vehicle approaching and switched off the flashlight as he dashed in the direction where he assumed the cave was. He hit his foot on a big rock but made it to the cave before the headlights of the truck illuminated the area. Another off-road vehicle followed the first one.

"Did they see you?" Adler asked, and looked at the Liberation Movement soldiers who stepped out of the vehicles.

"I don't think so, but they might have seen the light from the flashlight," Dennis said and crouched even more.

When the soldiers stepped into the headlights, Dennis saw that they were carrying machine guns. He had seen such poverty in Juba that he was pretty sure these soldiers were sponsored by some foreign country that had some interest in this area. Apparently, their military training was not in line with their modern equipment as they just looked around a while before returning to their vehicles.

"Amateurs," Adler said. "They don't even have flashlights."

"Yeah, but it seems like they can see here ... so no bonfire tonight," Dennis said sadly.

"It's gonna be fucking cold before the sun rises," Adler complained.

The ground in the cave was rock. They spread the grass to make it bit softer to sleep. Then they took off their wet and cold combat uniforms.

"Um ... we need to sleep closer," Adler said, shaking from cold.

"Better?" Dennis said as he shifted a bit closer. He knew what Adler meant but was hesitating.

"I mean ... really close," Adler said, pulling Dennis close to him.

Dennis felt how Adler put his hand around him. His Prince Charming was hugging him, and he sensed the heat from Adler's body. Simultaneously, the position made him nervous, and he was too afraid to move. Then he felt how his erection started to grow, though luckily Adler was behind him and could not feel it.

"Um … I'm not sure if this is the best moment, but … what you saw in the embassy…," Dennis said. He was not sure what to say, but he could not stay silent longer.

"You were kissing," Adler said. There was some tension in his voice.

"I guess you know it now, but I am…," Dennis said hesitantly.

"Gay," Adler completed the sentence.

"Yes," Dennis whispered.

They lay on the grass holding each other, and neither of them said anything for a while. Dennis feared that Adler would pull away or, even worse, discover his erection, which he was not able to will down.

"To be honest, I'm a bit disappointed," Adler said finally.

"I'm sorry. It's just how I am, but it doesn't have to change anything," Dennis said.

"No, I didn't mean that."

"What did you mean then?"

"I wish you had told me," Adler said. "You let me humiliate myself by trying to take you to a bar to find a girl."

"Oh…," Dennis said. "I wish I had said something. It just wasn't so easy."

"I understand," Adler said.

Dennis felt how Adler tightened the hold of his arm around him. He assumed it was a sign of acceptance, and he could not help smiling a bit. Their situation was severe. Without food and water, they would not survive many days, but at least Adler knew now and he seemed to be fine. It was all that mattered right now.

"Do you like him?"

"Who?" Dennis said.

"Dumbass." Adler snorted. "Jafar, of course."

"Huh? I guess I do," Dennis said and blushed. Fortunately, Adler could not see it.

"It was kind of obvious," Adler said. "You guys seemed to hang out together quite a lot," he added.

Adler moved a bit and, as he changed the position of arm, his elbow touched Dennis' erection. He laughed and moved his arm quickly away.

"I see you like cuddling with me," Adler said. Dennis was about to die of embarrassment.

Dennis lay there with his whole body tense. Even though he had dreamt of this moment many times, now than it was reality, he was ashamed. An awkward silence surrounded them, and Dennis was desperately thinking what he should say.

"Let's try to get some sleep, horny boy," Adler said finally.

"Ha-ha," Dennis said and tried to relax.

Soon Dennis heard Adler's steady breathing behind his back, and he fell asleep too, hoping that it was not their last night.

Chapter 9

Lieutenant Colonel Malcolm Davies pressed the doorbell. It was a nice morning in Northern California, almost too beautiful a morning for the task at hand. Soon an elegant lady in her fifties answered the door. She was not surprised to see a man in a Marines uniform standing at her door.

"Mrs. Benson?" Colonel Davies said and took his hat off his head.

"That's me," she said.

"Could I come in?" Colonel Davies said. "Is Mr. Benson at home, too?"

Mrs. Benson let him in and guided him to the kitchen where Mr. Benson was finishing his breakfast. When he saw Colonel Davies, he stood up and shook hands with the Marine.

"How can we help you?" Mrs. Benson asked. "Would you like some coffee?"

"No, thank you," Colonel Davies said. "It's about your son, Corporal Dennis Benson," he added, and sat down without waiting for an invitation.

"What has happened?" Mrs. Benson said, understanding that it was something serious.

"Your son … Corporal Benson … he died yesterday in an attack on the US Embassy in Juba in South Sudan," Colonel Davies said.

He had been the Commanding Officer for the First Reconnaissance Battalion for a decade, and delivered sad news dozens of times. Still, meeting the parents of a deceased young Marine was as difficult as the very first time he had delivered such a message.

"Could you please tell us how it happened?" Mrs. Benson said, tears running down her cheeks.

"We are still investigating," Colonel Davies said, reluctant to give them any further information.

"My poor baby. I can't believe this," Mrs. Benson sobbed.

"We will organize him a military funeral as soon as we have transferred the body to the US," Colonel Davis said.

Mrs. Benson was not listening. Her face was pale, and she held her hands in front of her mouth. Nothing mattered anymore. Nothing Colonel Davies said could bring Dennis back. They were just empty words.

"Ma'am, is there anything I can do?" Colonel Davies asked.

"Yes. I want my son alive," Mrs. Benson said bitterly, and glared at him.

"I understand," Colonel Davis, nodding.

He gave Mrs. Benson some papers to sign, and then he left. He had done his job, and it was time for him to return to Camp Pendleton, where he would oversee a big event where the Marine Corps recruited new young Marines to serve the country. For every loss, there were dozens of young Americans willing to test if they had better luck on the battlefield.

Once Colonel Davies had left, Mr. Benson opened the fridge and took out a bottle of beer. Then he turned on the television and sat down on the sofa. He had not said a word during the Colonel's visit, and his face had remained expressionless.

The familiar prayer call woke up Jafar on the morning following the explosion at the embassy. He felt irritated. The ritual he was expected to follow and the prayer he should say were not just religion. To Jafar, they represented the power that his father had over him.

Jafar took out the picture of Dennis that he'd hidden under his mattress and looked at it. *It was wrong, terribly wrong, but why did it feel so good?* he thought, recalling the moment they had spent in Dennis' room.

"What's that picture, and why aren't you praying?" Jafar heard Rabih asking.

"It's nothing," Jafar said to his brother, stuffing the picture back under his mattress.

"Wanna wash yourself first?" Rabih asked.

"Sure," Jafar said, unenthusiastically, and left the room.

Jafar had to sit down to wash himself. The image of Dennis in his mind made him hard, and he did not want anyone to see it. The water cleaned his body, but his mind felt dirty. *I'm a sodomite*, Jafar said to himself. It felt overwhelming, especially now when he had moved back to his father's house.

His whole life, Jafar had been taught how men were different from women and how he one day should marry a girl and have a family. And the entire time, Jafar had felt that something was wrong, but he had not known what it was. Now he knew, and it made him cry.

"Jafar, stop wasting the water. It's your brother's turn!" his father yelled from the back door.

"I'm sorry," Jafar said and covered himself with the small towel he had brought.

"And be home early today. We'll visit my brother at his farm after I've returned from work," Mr. Badri said as he closed the door.

"Great," Jafar said bitterly.

Soon the family was sitting on their pillows around the kitchen table. The women had cooked aseedas, and there were also fresh fruits. Jafar looked at the dumpling on his plate, unable to eat. *Why has God given me all these sinful thoughts?* he pondered, trying to force Dennis out of his mind.

After breakfast, Jafar walked to the mosque where he found a motorbike taxi that took him to the embassy. The events of the previous day made him nervous, but something forced him to go and see what was left of the embassy. He hoped that whoever had tried to kill him would not be there any longer.

When he arrived at the embassy, he saw that there was very little left of the main building. It was badly collapsed, as was the residence building. The walls of the medical center, which had been white, were now black and covered in dirt and soot. The scene was tragic.

Jafar walked to where the main gate had been and saw a Marine building up a fence. He approached the Marine cautiously, trying to get his attention.

"The embassy is closed," the Marine said.

"But I work here," Jafar said.

"The embassy is closed," the Marine repeated as he studied Jafar carefully.

"Is Corporal Benson here?" Jafar asked hopefully.

"Who?"

"Corporal Dennis Benson," Jafar said. "One of the Marines who came here some weeks ago," he added.

The Marine looked suspiciously at Jafar, who did not give up but waited for a reply. The answer surprised him.

"There is no Marine called Dennis Benson here. Besides, we just arrived here this morning," the Marine said.

"I mean the Marines who arrived here earlier. I want to know what happened to them," Jafar insisted.

"Look, boy, I don't know what you are talking about, but there were no Marines before us. Now get lost," the Marine said and gave Jafar an intimidating look.

Feeling miserable, Jafar left the Marine and walked along the street. His time in the embassy was over, and his dream of travelling to America had faded away. He would spend the rest of his life on a farm outside Juba, and if that was not bad enough, he had these disturbing feelings for other men and Dennis was not there to help him with them. *Either I keep them hidden, or I die*, Jafar analyzed his current situation.

The intimate moment with Dennis was something that could never happen again. Jafar wondered if it had all been just a big mistake. *Maybe God sent Dennis to test me, and I failed*, Jafar thought, feeling guilty. The mixed feelings stormed in his head.

Jafar walked to his car, which he had left parked near the embassy the previous night. It was even more damaged now. Some hooligans had stolen the front tires and broken all the windows. Aimlessly, he walked to the nearby park. He kept wandering until he found a shadow under a big tree and sat on the grass. The park was crowded, so he closed his eyes to be alone with his thoughts.

He tried to pray, but felt that nobody was listening. He tried again, but still got no answer, which made him more and more frustrated. The noises around him made it difficult to focus on anything, so he opened his eyes and saw a couple walking in the park. The girl was pretty, but she was nothing compared to the gorgeous young man walking hand in hand with her. Jafar's eyes lingered on him until he realized that he was staring at the man and turned his face away.

Dennis is gone, but Allah is sending more men to torment me, he thought frustrated. *How can I make this stop?*

With nowhere to go, Jafar decided to walk home. When he passed the university, he heard some gunshots and saw people running, but he did not care. *My life is ruined anyway*, he thought and kept walking. Tears started to fill his eyes, but he did not stop.

It took over an hour for Jafar to walk home. His mother had seen his coming and was standing in the kitchen. Her face was stringent.

"Come here," she said bluntly.

"What is it, Mother?" Jafar said and stepped closer timidly.

"I found this in your bed," she said, and showed Jafar the picture of Dennis.

"Um … that's Dennis, one of the Marines I told you about."

"I know what it is," she said firmly, "and I also know why you have it."

Jafar was shocked and did not know what to say. He stood quietly and waited for what his mother would say next. His heart was beating rapidly, and he felt it difficult to breathe.

"I've feared this for quite some time," she said with disgust in her voice.

"Let me explain—"

"I don't want to hear," she snapped.

"Okay," Jafar conceded with a small voice.

"You will marry the girl your father has chosen for you. And we will never speak of this again," she said determinedly.

She slammed the picture against Jafar's chest and told him to destroy it. Then she left the house to get water from the mosque. Jafar's sisters, who had been working in the garden, followed her. Jafar stood in the kitchen, staring at the picture. He knew that he should throw it away, but he could not do it. Even if Dennis were still alive, he would return to the US after his mission. They would never meet again. Jafar wanted to keep his only memento of that fabled encounter, so he hid the picture in his wallet.

Jafar tensed when he heard his father returning from work some hours later. He moved closer to the door of his bedroom so that he could hear what his parents would discuss. He listened carefully, so scared that he forgot to breathe, but she did not mention the picture.

After waiting awhile, Jafar went to the living room and found his father sitting on the chair. Jafar's mother had just served him coffee, and she glared at Jafar when he approached his father.

"Father, I've been thinking," Jafar said hesitantly.

"Leave thinking to people who are smarter than you," Mr. Badri said.

Jafar was not sure whether his father was joking, or was still mad at him because of the broken car. His father did not often joke, but on the other hand, it was not Jafar's fault that the embassy had been attacked the previous day. For better or worse, Jafar decided to continue.

"We're gonna visit my uncle today, right?" Jafar said.

"That's correct. And your bride, Amira, will be there, too," Mr. Badri said.

"Well ... if you don't mind, I would like to stay there," Jafar said, and studied his father's reaction.

When the silence stretched, Jafar explained, "I mean, I've quit my job at the embassy, and they should have the room ready for me ... and my wife."

Jafar saw a smile on his mother's face as his own stomach turned.

"We can ask my brother, but that should be okay," Mr. Badri said.

"Thanks, Father," Jafar said.

"But it means that your wedding will be this weekend," Mr. Badri said, "and you are not going to sleep with Amira before that."

"Um ... that's okay, Father," Jafar said. The thought of sleeping with Amira made him feel uncomfortable.

Jafar felt alleviated. Had his mother told his father about the picture and her presumption that he was gay, his life would be in danger. Jafar had heard rumors that some years ago the Muslim community in Hai Jalaba had stoned to death a group of young men who were assumed to be homosexuals. If Jafar was lucky, he would leave his family tonight.

"Jafar," his mother said when he was walking back to his bedroom.

"Yes, Mother," Jafar said, turning to look at his mother.

"Pack everything you need," she said, "and throw away what you don't need."

She gave Jafar a meaningful look that sent chills down his spine. He returned quickly to his bedroom and started to pack his clothes in a big bag. The picture of Dennis was still in his wallet, and he planned to keep it there.

There was not much to pack, so soon he had his properties in the bag. As he took a final glimpse of the bedroom where he had slept twenty-one years of his life, he saw the embassy cellphone on the table. The Chief of Staff had given it to him when the evacuation started, but with the embassy badly damaged and closed, Jafar did not know what to do with the phone. Finally, he decided to pack the phone in his bag.

"Ready to start your new life? I heard that you're moving to the farm today," Abdul said as he walked into the room.

"I guess so." Jafar hugged his older brother. "I'm gonna miss you and my nephews."

"We'll keep visiting you," Abdul said, taken aback by Jafar's expression of emotions.

Abdul had lived at the same farm when he had married Amira's sister five years ago. Once Abdul had made enough money working at the bank with their father, he and his wife had moved to their own apartment in Juba. Abdul was now an associate manager, and his wife was at home with their two boys.

"How is it at the farm?" Jafar asked.

"Well, to be honest, compared to Juba, it's a rat hole in the middle of nowhere," Abdul said.

"Thanks for the encouragement," Jafar said, picking up his bag.

"C'mon, it's time for you to become a man." Abdul laughed and punched Jafar on his arm.

As the brothers walked out, Jafar realized that he no longer had a car. The farm was dozens of miles from Juba; without his car, he would be literally stuck there.

"But how do I get there? My car is at the embassy, and it's broken," Jafar said.

"I'll drive you there. You won't need a car at the farm," Mr. Badri said.

"Yes, Father," Jafar said, disappointed.

"And the women will clean the house," Mr. Badri said to Jafar's mother and youngest sister, who were standing at the door.

Abdul took his own car, and Jafar drove with his father. They drove nearly thirty miles north and then turned right onto a narrow gravel road that led toward the White Nile River. It took them almost an hour, but finally they arrived at the farm, which was located near the river. It was already dark, but Jafar could see a small house in the headlights. His uncle was standing in front of the house waiting for them.

Mr. Badri greeted his brother, and Jafar and Abdul followed them to the house. Amira was sitting on a sofa and smiled shyly to Jafar, who studied his new home. He had been there before, but it felt different now.

"Your father said you would like to move here," Jafar's uncle said.

"He's a grown man. He's not returning to his mother," Mr. Badri said, ignoring Jafar, who was about to say something.

"Well, in that case, it's agreed then," Jafar's uncle said.

"I want you to organize their marriage for this weekend," Mr. Badri said to his brother.

"Is that okay with you?" Jafar's uncle said, turning to look at Jafar.

"Yes, it is," Mr. Badri said.

"We need to celebrate this," Jafar's uncle said and took a bottle of cheap araqi from the cupboard.

Officially, sharia banned the consumption of alcohol, but apparently even Mr. Badri was allowed to take a break from his religion. Jafar's father, uncle, and brother kept drinking the gin like it was some sort of a competition. Once the bottle was empty, Jafar's uncle brought out a new one. After each glass, Mr. Badri blessed God, and soon the three men were singing songs that Jafar did not recognize. Amira's two younger sisters and their mother tried, in vain, to sleep in the next room.

"You don't like it?" Abdul said to Jafar, who was still holding his first glass in his hand.

"Huh?" Jafar said, looking at the glass.

"I wonder, little brother, if you are a real man at all," Abdul said. Jafar heard from his voice that he was drunk.

Jafar did not say anything but looked at Amira sitting next to him. She looked uncomfortable, like she was afraid of the drunk men.

"Are you a man?" Abdul said, raising his voice.

"Yes," Jafar said in a voice that was barely louder than a whisper.

"I can't hear you," Abdul said. "Are you a real man?"

Jafar tensed but kept quiet. He watched as Abdul rose from the chair, staggered toward him, and kept asking if he was a real man. His father and uncle were watching and laughing. Jafar found the situation irrational, but it became soon threatening when his brother tried to hit him.

"Please stop," Jafar said. He was now standing and moved away from his brother.

"Please stop," Abdul imitated in a mocking tone.

"Don't hurt him," Amira said.

"Oh," Abdul said, surprised, and turned to look at Amira. "You need a girl to defend you," he said to Jafar, who heard his father and uncle laughing again.

"Maybe I need to show your girl who's a real man," Abdul blustered and stared at Amira with madness and lust in his eyes.

Amira had just turned fourteen, which was the best age for girls to marry. Most boys wanted a young wife, and in just a year or two, she would become a burden to her father. Jafar assumed that was the reason he had been chosen to marry Amira, rather than his being an ideal candidate in his uncle's eyes.

Abdul took hold of Amira with one hand while the other was pulling down his pants. He was heavily drunk, and his efforts to take off his pants were not successful. He had to release his hold on Amira to open his belt. Jafar's uncle poured more araqi for himself and his brother, ignoring what was happening to his daughter.

"Stop. I don't want that!" Amira said and stood up as soon as Abdul released his hold on her.

"Who asked your opinion?" Abdul stepped closer.

"She's mine," Jafar said, moving between Abdul and Amira. He had to act before his drunken brother could do something to Amira.

"So you're a man, after all," Abdul said, laughing.

"Yes," Jafar said.

"Prove it," Abdul said. "Fuck your girl."

Jafar looked at his brother, frightened. Abdul was bigger than he was, and he had never seen Abdul behaving like this. Jafar saw his father and uncle sitting on the sofa and singing. Amira had backed to the corner of the room, apparently scared. Jafar tried to think how to get out of the situation. He had no intention of having sex with a fourteen-year-old girl in front of his brother and father.

"Fuck your bitch," Abdul said again.

"Not before we are married," Jafar said. "Sex before marriage is a sin."

Abdul looked at him in confusion. Then he burst out laughing and shook his head. He tried to sip from his glass, but it was empty. He had spilled all his gin on the floor.

"Whatever," Abdul said finally. "I need more of this." He took the bottle from the table.

Jafar sighed. In his mind, he thanked Allah for saving him from a situation that would have soon become more than awkward. *Maybe religion is not all bad after all*, he thought.

Abdul tried to pour himself more araqi but managed to get more on the table than in his glass. Then he sat back in his chair and joined his father and uncle in the song they were singing. In half an hour, all three men were sleeping on their seats.

"There's a bed for you in the shed," Amira said softly to Jafar. "I'll take your bag and show you the way."

"Thanks," Jafar said as he took an oil lamp from the table and followed her to a small shed near the house.

Amira opened the door, which did not have a lock, and they stepped into the shed. It was just one room, but in the dim light of the lamp, Jafar found it cozy. There was a table, a small cupboard for his clothes, and a bed that was barely big enough for two. It reminded him of the room at the embassy where he and Dennis had touched each other.

"Do you need anything?" Amira asked, placing Jafar's bag next to the bed.

"Huh? No, thanks," Jafar said. "I'm tired. It's been quite a day."

Amira laughed nervously. "Okay, good night then," she said, and then left.

"Good night," Jafar said, but Amira could not hear him any longer.

Silence filled the small room. It was almost too silent for Jafar, who was used to life in busy Juba. He took his clothes from the bag and put them in the cupboard. He hoped his uncle would have some working clothes for him.

Jafar's cellphone beeped in his bag, indicating that the battery was almost dead. He took the phone and the charger, but noticed there were no sockets to connect the charger. The phone beeped again, and then it hit him. *There's no electricity—and no network either*, he thought and put the useless phone back in his bag.

Feeling lonely and isolated, Jafar tried not to think about Dennis. He felt an urge to take the picture from his wallet but forced himself to turn out the oil lamp before the temptation became too strong. Lying on the bed, he closed his eyes and fell asleep, hoping that his father and brother would be gone when he woke up.

Chapter 10

Someone was sneaking in the cave. Dennis saw a shadow on the wall and was sure that it was a human. Hoping it was not too late, he turned to find his pistol, but could not remember where he had left it the previous night. Then he heard a voice.

"Morning, sunshine," Adler said.

"Huh? Oh, it's you," Dennis said, and fell back on the grass bedding and rubbed his eyes. "Did you sleep well?"

"No. I'm not used to sleeping with guys," Adler said with a grin.

"Ha-ha," Dennis said, feeling a bit self-conscious.

"Actually, my ankle is killing me. I hardly slept at all," Adler said. Dennis recognized the serious tone in his voice.

Adler had moved to the mouth of the cave where the sun was shining. The night had been cold, and he tried to get warm in the sunlight. Dennis was shaking from cold, too, so he joined Adler in the sun.

"The temperature is rising rapidly. We might need to wait here in the shadow until it gets dark," Adler said.

"Yeah. Without water, we will die out there," Dennis said, studying the horizon.

From where they had come, as far as they could see, there was just savanna. In the direction where they assumed Abyei Town was, it was nothing but rocks and sand. Farther out, there were some hills, and Dennis hoped the town would be behind them. What worried him was that he could not see a single tree that would give them any shade.

"Do you hear anything? Anything at all?" Adler said.

"No. Should I?" Dennis said.

"If there were people living near us, we should hear some noises," Adler said, and Dennis understood what he meant.

"Shit," Dennis said.

As soon as their bodies had warmed up, they crawled again to the back of the cave where the sun was not shining. They had only one bottle of water, so they had to be careful not to sweat. Surviving without food, even several days, was easy. Preventing dehydration was the tricky thing.

"May I ask something?" Adler said tentatively after they had been sitting in the cave for fifteen minutes.

"Sure. I guess we don't have much to do for several hours," Dennis said.

"Your argument with your parents. Is it about you being ... you know ... gay?"

"Um, yes." Dennis felt suddenly tongue-tied.

"Oh, sorry, it's none of my business. You don't have to talk about it," Adler said.

"No. It's just ... complicated."

Dennis told Adler how his parents had kicked him out of their home on Christmas Eve a year ago. Adler listened quietly and felt sorry for his teammate. He tried to imagine how it must have felt for Dennis.

"I could never do that to my child," Adler said when Dennis had finished.

"Nobody should," Dennis said, and sighed.

"A friend of mine came out during our senior year in high school. It was no issue at all, not to his parents or anybody," Adler said.

"You said you went to Lowell High School?" Dennis said.

"Yeah, but don't think that I'm open-minded just because I grew up in San Francisco," Adler said.

Adler's comment made Dennis smile. He had been so worried about his teammates finding out that he was gay. Of course, he should have known that Adler was not just a tough sergeant but a smart guy and a loyal friend. He had lost the opportunity to tell Newton and Mullen, but if he had to spend his last days here, it felt comforting that he had shared his secret with someone.

"How does it feel to be gay?" Adler asked. "I mean in the Marine Corps."

"Don't ask; don't tell," Dennis snorted.

"I always thought that policy was bullshit."

"You did?" Dennis asked.

"I don't know about the guys in the Army, but Marines should know that some people are straight and some are gay," Adler said. "Even kids in fucking elementary school know that much."

"I see your point," Dennis said with a smile. "You think Newton and Mullen would have been okay with it?"

"For sure. They were great kids," Alder said.

They had been sitting in the cave for three hours when they heard the sound of an engine behind the hills. They quickly grabbed their uniforms that had been drying in the sun and hid them in the cave so they could not be seen from outside. Then they moved to the back of the cave and lay on the ground. Soon one of the off-road vehicles they had seen the day before appeared behind the hills.

"I don't think they can see us. The mouth of the cave is small, and there are no signs of anybody being here," Dennis said.

"I just wish we had had time to put on our uniforms," Adler said.

"Maybe this is a good distraction," Dennis said.

"Yeah, they don't expect to find two half-naked guys in this cave," Adler half-joked.

"They don't, and that gives us time to shoot them," Dennis said, gripping the handle of his Glock.

"Maybe you're right," Adler said.

"I'm always right."

The truck drove quite close to them, but it did not stop. Instead, it continued to the site of the helicopter crash. There were two men sitting in the cabin and four or five on the bed. They had their machine guns with them again.

"Do you think they know we survived the crash, or are they just patrolling here?" Dennis said.

"No idea. But you said they might have seen your flashlight," Adler said.

"Should we try to ambush them? There are only six or seven."

"And there are only two of us with handguns," Adler said. "We have a better chance of staying alive if they don't know about us."

The midday sun was hot, and the Marines were sweating heavily despite their effort to stay still in the shadows of the cave. When the sun finally set, they had emptied the water bottle. Dennis felt thirsty, and not eating anything made him weak.

"Do you have Aquatabs?" Adler asked.

"I think so," Dennis said, and took a small box of water purification tablets from his pocket.

"If we find water that is clean enough, we could fill your bottle and use them to make the water safer to drink," Adler said.

"Can we piss in the bottle and use these to clean it?" Dennis said, studying the directions with his flashlight.

"Well, basically that would be safer to drink than dirty water, but the taste is fucking awful," Adler said. "I would use that as a plan B."

"Sounds like a plan ... B," Dennis said.

Adler switched on the GSP and waited until it got the signal before he entered the coordinates of Abyei Town. In a couple of seconds, the device advised them to move twenty miles to the northeast. Had the sun still be shining, Dennis would have seen the desperation in Adler's face.

"It's too far away," Adler said.

"What do you mean?"

"I can't walk twenty miles with this fucking ankle," Adler said. "You should go alone."

"And leave you here to die?" Dennis said, raising his voice. "No fucking way."

"I can't walk. I would just slow you down."

"Shut up. I'll carry you if I have to. Let's go."

They kept walking slowly, checking every now and then from the GPS that they were moving to the right direction. The bones in Adler's ankle seemed to be severely broken, and he could not put pressure on his right foot at all. Dennis had to support his every step.

They reached the hill they had seen from the cave, and climbed cumbersomely to the top. It was hard to move in the darkness with just a small flashlight, especially when they were constantly worried that somebody might see the light.

"Um ... I need to take a leak," Adler said.

"Wanna pee in the bottle?" Dennis asked.

He felt uncomfortable with the idea of drinking Adler's piss, but they had walked almost two hours and had not seen a single drop of water. He was thirsty after helping the heavy sergeant to move, and when the sun rose, they would not survive another day without drinking.

"I guess I should," Adler said tentatively.

"Okay," Dennis said, and gave the bottle to Adler.

"Um ... could you hold me and shine the light?"

"Huh?" Dennis said even as he pointed the light at Adler's crotch.

"And turn your head," Adler said. "Not gonna give you any freak show."

Dennis laughed and waited while Adler filled the bottle. He looked around carefully but could not see a single light in the darkness of the night. It was getting colder, but this time their clothes were dry. Besides, the exercise he got from walking Adler kept him warm.

"Ew! It's warm. This is so fucking gross," Dennis said when Adler gave him the bottle back.

"Sorry, don't have ice cubes for your cocktail," Adler said.

"I put in a couple of tablets in case we really need to drink this," Dennis said.

After walking another two or three hours, the savanna started again. Soon they found some buildings that looked abandoned. A small sparkle of hope bubbled in their minds. Then they saw a military truck parked in front of one of the buildings.

"Wait here. I'll check the truck," Dennis said, helping Adler to sit against the building.

"Be careful," Adler said. "The men we saw might have a camp here."

"I'm always careful." Dennis switched off the flashlight.

He sneaked slowly in the direction where he thought the truck was. In the darkness, he could hardly see anything, but he did not want to risk someone seeing the light from the flashlight. Fumbling with his arms, he finally found the truck.

Fearing somebody might find him at any moment, Dennis walked to the other side of the truck and tried the right front door. It was not locked, so he carefully pulled it open. As soon as he got it open, the bright lights in the cabin switched on. Dennis rushed into the cabin and searched for the light switch in panic but could not find it.

Then he realized that the cabin light would turn off if he closed the door.

The darkness returned, and Dennis sat silently in the cabin, listening to his heartbeat. He waited a couple of minutes but still could not see or hear anything. Either his enemy was approaching him in the darkness, or nobody had seen him entering the truck. The situation made him nervous.

Finally, Dennis felt safe to switch on the flashlight. Blocking most of the light with his hand, he searched the cabin. He found no guns or other military equipment, but his gut feeling told him that the truck belonged to the Liberation Movement. Then he saw something that made him happier than the Christmas presents he had received when he was a small kid. There were two water bottles in the glove box.

"Holy shit," Adler said when Dennis returned and showed him the water he had found.

"Yeah, we can throw away your gourmet drink," Dennis said.

"Did you see any place we could sleep?" Adler asked.

"There is a small stall a bit farther away from the other building," Dennis said. "It looks abandoned."

"Great, help me there," Adler said. Despite his broken ankle, the water clearly improved his mood.

Adler waited at the door while Dennis walked around the stall one more time to make sure that there were no Liberation Movement soldiers. As he did not see anything or anybody, they stepped carefully into the old stall. The floor was covered with hay, and there was a pungent smell of animals. They searched the small room with the flashlight, but they found nothing bigger than a rat.

"This will do," Adler said.

"You're such a modest guy," Dennis teased. "I was expecting some five-star hotel."

"It'll be morning soon, but should we try to sleep a bit?"

"Good idea, I'm exhausted," Dennis said.

"You sleep first. I'll keep watch," Adler offered.

Dennis did not argue. He lay down on the hay and closed his eyes. The temperature had decreased, and he felt cold lying on the floor, but he could not find the courage to ask Adler to keep him warm. Besides, he was not sure if his desire to have Adler close was just because of the coldness or whether he would have had some ulterior motives.

The next morning, Dennis woke when Adler poked his shoulder. He opened his eyes and saw Adler giving him a sign to be silent.

"There are people walking outside," Adler whispered.

"Did you see them? How many?" Dennis breathed.

"No, but we need to hide."

Dennis looked around the small room. It looked different now when the sunlight came in from the small windows near the roof. There was nothing except four walls, the windows, and a door that led to the yard where the people were walking. The men outside were talking, but the Marines did not understand the language.

"There isn't really anyplace to hide," Dennis said.

"Then let's just hope they don't come in here," Adler said.

"Why should they? There's nothing in here."

They sat on the opposite corners of the stall and targeted the door with their guns. The engine of the truck started, which made it more difficult for the Marines to hear if somebody was coming into their hiding place. Then they heard the truck drive off. They waited until the sound of the engine faded.

"I can't hear anything," Dennis said, shifting forward to carefully open the door.

"Can you see anybody?" Adler whispered.

"No," Dennis said. "Wait here. I'll go and check." He disappeared through the door.

There were three small, one-floor buildings, and Dennis saw them now for the first time in sunlight. He approached the first building from the direction where there were no windows. When he got to the building, he sneaked around the corner and looked inside a window. The room was small, and several beds and mattresses were scattered across the floor. The guys who had just left must have slept there.

Dennis walked to the next window and saw a similar bedroom, but it looked like nobody had slept there for a while. If there were Liberation Movement soldiers living here, there could not be more than six or seven.

The second building was even smaller, and it did not have any windows. Dennis walked to the door and tried to open it, but it was locked. The lock looked rather simple, so he decided to break it. He took a stone from the ground, but on his way back to the door, he heard somebody singing.

Dennis hid quickly behind the corner of the building. Just then, an old woman came from the third building carrying a big black cauldron. A small girl followed her and sang with a fragile voice. Luckily, they did not see Dennis.

The old woman said something to the girl. Then she hung the cauldron over a fire pit and started the fire. The woman and the girl filled the cauldron with water from the nearby well. Finally, the old woman went to the building with the two bedrooms and emerged carrying a big pile of clothes.

Dennis watched from his hiding place when the old woman started to wash the clothes in the cauldron. The girl was playing with something that Dennis did not recognize at first. When the girl came closer, he realized that it was a hand grenade.

The girl could not have been much older than five. It troubled Dennis that such a young child was playing with weapons. However, he did not have much time to think about that since the girl was coming closer and closer while playing with the grenade. He looked back but could not find a place to hide. He was forced to move behind the next corner, even though he was sure the girl would see him changing position. She did.

For a short moment, Dennis and the girl stared at each other. Then Dennis took his battle knife and pointed it toward the girl. Just as Dennis had hoped, she screamed and ran to the old woman. Dennis used the opportunity to climb through the window into the third building. Soon, the old lady and the girl came behind the building, but they could not see Dennis anymore.

Dennis was now in some kind of kitchen. He saw vegetables and bread on the table, and he quickly put them in a bag he found. It would be their first meal for quite some time, but before they could enjoy it, Dennis had to find a way to return to the stall. If the old woman believed that the girl had seen somebody, they would soon come to look for him.

Should I just kill them? If I let them live, they will tell the Liberation Movement that they saw me, Dennis thought as he took his pistol from the holster. Suddenly he wished that Adler were there to tell him what he should do. He saw the small girl's scared face in his mind, and he decided to put his gun back. He was a Marine, not a murderer.

Dennis found some water bottles in the cupboard and added them to the bag with the vegetables and bread. Then he walked out of the building, thinking that the old woman and little girl would not be any threat to him. He was surprised when he could not see anybody in the yard.

What Dennis did not notice was that the door to the locked building was now open. The old woman came out with a machine gun and opened fire on Dennis, who was able to escape inside the building at the very last moment. Luckily for him, the old woman was not a very good shooter. He took his gun and prepared to act when he heard a gunshot.

"Target down!" Adler shouted.

Dennis came out and saw the old woman lying dead on the ground. The girl was screaming hysterically. When Dennis came closer, she ran to the building with the bedrooms and slammed the door behind her. Dennis heard the door lock from inside.

"We need to go," Adler said as soon as Dennis had returned to the stall.

"I know, but let's eat some breakfast first. We have not eaten for more than a day," Dennis said, showing Adler what he had taken from the kitchen.

"Man, that's awesome. But let's be quick."

They ate and left. Adler's ankle was, if possible, even worse, and Dennis had to help him walk. The sun was shining from a clear sky and the temperature had rocketed to 95 degrees, but they had no choice. Besides, now they had water so they were not in immediate danger of dehydration. Still, they had to be careful.

After an hour of walking, they started to see more and more buildings. What was strange was that they all looked empty. There were no people anywhere, which of course made their escape easier, but it felt odd.

"The Liberation Movement has destroyed the entire town," Adler said.

"Huh?"

"Don't you get it? This is Abyei Town," Adler pointed out.

"But there is nobody living here," Dennis protested.

"That's exactly what I meant."

"Oh," Dennis said. "Why?"

"Don't ask me. I'm just a Marine sergeant," Adler said, "but this is fucking creepy. There should be thousands of people living here."

They heard sounds of incoming cars and hid in the long grass near the road. Soon, five off-road vehicles full of soldiers drove by and then turned to the yard of the biggest building in the deserted center of the town.

"You see that white two-floor building where the cars stopped?" Adler said.

"Yes, that's the same building from the pictures Captain Mills and General Christensen showed us," Dennis said.

"They assumed Shaker Salih lives there," Adler said.

"So, we did find our target."

"Too bad we aren't in a condition to finish the mission," Adler mused.

He was right. They had lost two Marines and most of their equipment when their helicopter had been shot down. In addition, Adler could not walk with his ankle, and it hurt so badly that he had not slept for two nights. Dennis felt weak after drinking and eating so little. Besides, they would soon need to find more food and water, which was not easy in a deserted town where the only inhabitants were enemy soldiers.

"Let's go to that building over there," Adler said. "We should be able to sleep there tonight."

"But aren't they looking for us?"

"It's possible that they found the dead woman already," Adler said.

"And the girl will tell them about us," Dennis added.

"Possibly, but they still don't know where we are."

"So, let's sleep and hope they don't find us," Dennis said, finishing Adler's thought.

The building was empty, like they had expected, but it looked like whoever had lived there had just disappeared without taking anything with them. There was some bread in the kitchen, but it was covered with mold. Dennis found clothes drying in the backyard.

They ate some fruit and drank one of their water bottles. Then they started to prepare for the night. Adler hung a couple of empty metal cans against the door so that they would create some noise if anyone opened the door. It had to be loud enough to wake them, but not too complicated to look like it was planned to work that way.

"We could sleep in the kitchen. There, under the table," Dennis said, pointing.

"Not a bad idea. They can't see us from the windows," Adler said.

"Wait here. I'll get some blankets."

Dennis went to the other room and gathered up an armload of blankets. He built them a cozy place to sleep beneath the table, which blocked visibility from the window. He even pushed the cupboard in a way that it gave them some shield if anyone looked from the door to the kitchen. There was not much room, but they both appreciated the safety it provided. When the sun set, they lay shoulder to shoulder.

"I don't get this. We are in Africa, but it's freaking cold in here," Dennis said.

"If you don't mind, let's keep each other warm," Adler said as he turned and put his arm around Dennis.

"Hmm … why should I mind?" Dennis said, smiling to himself and moving closer. "I just thought you had a wife at home."

"Don't get any ideas," Adler said. "I'm still straight."

Adler was quiet for some time, obviously thinking about something. Dennis wanted to ask what it was, but he knew that he had to give Adler time to gather his thoughts.

"I wonder what happened to that girl," Adler said finally.

"You regret shooting that old lady?"

"Yes and no," Adler said. "If I hadn't, she might have killed you."

"That's possible," Dennis said.

"I just can't stop thinking what will happen to the girl."

"We left her alive, which I think was the right decision. The rest is not in our control," Dennis said. "Besides, one of the men there must be her father."

"Maybe you are right," Adler allowed. "And maybe we should try to sleep now."

"I'm always right," Dennis said.

It was the first night since the helicopter crash that Dennis slept well. He did not even wake up when the sun rose and lightened the kitchen. Finally, Adler had to wake him up.

"I need to pee like a racehorse," Adler said.

"Okay, let me help you out," Dennis said as he rolled from beneath the table.

When he glanced at Adler, he gasped in shock. Adler was pale, and the skin around his eyes was black. He looked much older than twenty-six—and very sick. Dennis helped Adler up and noticed that he had to take hold of the wall with both hands to keep standing.

"You look sick," Dennis said.

"I haven't slept for three nights," Adler said.

"Your ankle is that bad?"

"Worse," Adler admitted. "I need to see a doctor soon."

"Then we'll leave today," Dennis said.

"How?" Adler asked.

"I don't know yet," Dennis said. "But we'll leave today," he added with determination in his voice.

Adler spent the day on the bed that Dennis had set up in the kitchen while they talked about their options. They could try to steal a car from the Liberation Movement, but it felt risky and, without a map, they did not know where to drive. Their military GPS was not especially designed to give route instructions. Their other choice was to find a telephone so they could call the Special Operations Command and ask for help. They decided to try the second option.

As soon as it got dark, they left the house where they had slept and walked to the building where they had seen the cars going the previous day. There were lights on in the building, and some of the cars were parked out front. However, there were fewer cars than the day before, and they hoped that was a good sign.

"Should we try that building first? It's probably empty," Adler said, pointing toward a smaller building near the big one.

"Yeah, let's try it," Dennis said, helping Adler to the door.

They went in, and Dennis used the flashlight to search the only room in the building. It was some kind of office.

In the middle of the room was a table with some papers piled on it—right beside a telephone.

Dennis rushed to the phone and entered the number for the Special Operations Command Emergency Center. He waited patiently, but as soon as the call was connected, he heard some recording. He was not sure of the language but thought it could be Arabic. He tried a couple of times, but the call was always connected to the same recording. Then he tried to call Camp Pendleton and even his parents, but the result was the same.

"The phone's not working," Dennis said, disappointed.

"Or maybe international calls are blocked," Adler said.

"But I don't know any local number, not even the number to the embassy."

The situation frustrated Dennis. He felt that they were so close, but then at the last possible moment everything was ruined. He cursed and thought feverishly what to do. Then he realized that he had a local number.

"Jafar," he said, and checked his pocket to see if he still had the number to Jafar's cellphone.

"He must be in the embassy, and he can contact the ambassador," Adler said, delighted.

Dennis found the number and called it. It took several long seconds before the phone started to ring, and just then two armed soldiers walked into the room. He saw how the first solder raised his gun and pointed it at him. The phone kept ringing, but it did not matter anymore.

Chapter 11

Sweat was streaming down his face and body. Jafar had been weeding the vegetable garden the entire day. Finally, when the sun was setting, his uncle had allowed him to stop. He had not eaten anything, but he had an icky feeling in his stomach. The water that his uncle had brought him had been hardly clean.

"Jafar," his uncle called just as he was opening the door of the shed where he slept.

"Yes, Uncle?" Jafar said, fearing that his uncle had more tasks for him.

"Dinner will be ready soon. Amira made some porridge."

"Thanks, Uncle," Jafar said. Despite the sick feeling in his stomach, he thought he should try to eat something.

"Um … just one thing. Can I wash myself somewhere?" Jafar asked.

"Wash yourself?" his uncle said, and laughed. "The River Nile is one mile that direction," he said, pointing.

"Um … thanks," Jafar said, disappointed.

"I won't recommend going there now. It's getting dark, and the crocodiles might be hungry." His uncle laughed.

Jafar had not expected a five-star hotel—actually, he had never seen one and did not even know that such existed—but suddenly he missed his life in his father's house. Unlike his father, his uncle was poor. The farm was old and in bad shape, and the family could afford only one meal a day. And even that seemed to be mostly porridge.

Uncle must have sold Amira to get some money, Jafar thought. Typically, the father of the groom had to pay a significant amount of money to the bride's family. Then he realized it. *Father wanted to get rid of me, and uncle needed money*, he thought, and felt humiliated.

"I need to get away from here," Jafar said to himself as he took his bag from the floor.

His car was broken, so he could not just jump in his car and drive to Juba. Feeling desperate, Jafar tried to switch on his mobile phone, but it had run out of battery. Then he remembered that the farm had no electricity, and even if he could have charged the phone, there was no network coverage in the countryside. He was trapped.

Jafar took the picture of Dennis from his wallet. What he felt for the boy was wrong, it was a sin, but he needed something that would make him happy. *God sent me here to punish me for my sins*, Jafar thought, looking at the picture. He could not help thinking how beautiful Dennis was in the picture. Finally, he put the picture carefully back in his wallet. It felt like the picture was the only valuable thing he had left in the world.

When Jafar opened the door to the house, he noticed that the others were already eating. Amira rose from the table and brought Jafar a plate full of the porridge she had made.

"Do you like it?" Amira asked shyly when Jafar tasted the porridge.

"It's good," Jafar lied. The porridge was awful, but he could hardly blame Amira for that. Quite likely, it was the best that one could make out of the available ingredients.

"Thanks," Amira said with a smile.

"It's your welcoming meal," his uncle said.

"Um … thanks," Jafar said, unable to understand why his uncle sounded so angry.

"But tomorrow you need to work harder if you want to eat at my table."

"Yes, sir, I'll do my best," Jafar said, embarrassed.

Amira kept her face down. She could not look at Jafar or her father. Her two younger sisters played with the porridge and giggled at each other.

"Shut up and stop playing with the food!" Jafar's uncle took one of the cups the girls were playing with and threw the porridge on them.

The girls went first silent, but soon they started to cry silently. Their mother cleaned most of the porridge from their faces and hair, and took them to the other room. Jafar could see from her face that she feared her husband.

"Keep eating," the uncle said to nobody in particular.

"Um … this is so good," Jafar said quietly.

The uncle sighed and left the table. He walked out and slammed the door behind him. Jafar was not sure if he had done something wrong, but he definitely felt he had. Then his uncle's wife returned to the kitchen and looked at Jafar sympathetically.

"Don't worry, Jafar. The way he behaves, it's my fault," she said.

"What do you mean?" Jafar said.

"He wanted boys, but I gave him four girls," she said.

"Oh," Jafar said. He looked at Amira and felt a connection. He knew how it felt to be an unwanted child.

"He is jealous of your father," she said. "Your father is a wealthy man and has three sons."

He has two sons, and then he has me, Jafar thought. Everything is his life felt wrong. It was as if he had not found his place in the big world. He had lived only when he had worked in the embassy. Everything else had been just surviving. And then there was Dennis, who had disappeared from his life as suddenly as he had appeared in the first place.

"You will soon get married, and one day you can leave this farm and live happily together," his uncle's wife said.

"That sounds nice," Jafar said. Then he realized that she had not been talking about marrying Dennis but marrying Amira.

Jafar finished his meal, thanked Amira and her mother one more time, and left for the shed, hoping that he would not walk into his uncle on the way.

The wedding ceremony took place in Juba the following Saturday. It was a traditional Muslim ceremony. The banquet hall, which was full of beautiful decorations, was glorious, but Jafar was sure that his father had organized and paid for it just to impress his friends and relatives.

Jafar was dressed in white pants and a long purple jacket. He had a turban on his head, and his father had loaned him some jewels to wear. Jafar had borrowed the clothes from his brother, and they were a bit too big for him, which made him look even smaller than he was.

Amira walked in wearing a dress that was simple but pretty. Women were expected to dress modestly in Islam. Jafar guided her through the big ballroom to a smaller salon, where the female guests were waiting for the ceremony to start. Then he returned to the room where the men were sitting.

"According to the teachings of the Quran, both husband and wife are each other's protector and comforter. Thus, they are meant for one another," Mr. Badri said with a voice that could be heard in both rooms.

All guests went silent. Jafar kept staring at his pompous father who was, needless to say, enjoying the attention he was getting.

"For Muslim men and women, for believing men and women, for true men and women," Mr. Badri preached and looked at Jafar.

Jafar looked away. For a short moment, he was sure that his father knew what had happened with Dennis. Then he thought that is was just his guilty mind playing tricks on him. He turned his face back toward his father.

"For men and women who are patient, and for men and women who guard their chastity, and for men and women who engage much in Allah's praise, for them has Allah prepared forgiveness and great reward," Mr. Badri continued, quoting Chapter 33, Verse 35.

Once Mr. Badri had finished his speech, he approached his brother and gestured him to stand up.

"My dear brother, I'll ask the hand of your beautiful daughter to marry my son," Mr. Badri said.

"I'll promise her hand to your son," Mr. Badri's brother said.

"The mahr will be 8,000 pounds."

"Thank you for your generosity," his brother answered.

There were sounds of astonishment in the room. In Islamic tradition, a mahr was the payment the groom's father paid to the bride's father, but Jafar realized that the sum his father had to pay to get him married was exceptionally high. It was likely more than his uncle earned in a year.

Mr. Badri took the marriage contract from the table and asked Jafar to follow him to the room where Amira and the other women were. He put the contract in front of Amira.

"I've come to an agreement with your father. You can sign the contract now," Mr. Badri said.

Amira took the pen from Jafar's father and wrote her name quickly on the paper. Then she gave the pen to Jafar and waited until he had signed it, too. As soon as Jafar had done it, Mr. Badri took the paper, folded it, and put it in his pocket.

"Time for the vows," Mr. Badri said drily.

"I, Amira, offer you myself in marriage in accordance with the instructions of the Holy Quran and the Holy Prophet, peace and blessing be upon him. I pledge, in honesty and with sincerity, to be for you an obedient and faithful wife," Amira said.

Jafar looked at her and saw her smiling sweetly. Everything in her kept saying that she was having the moment of her life. Jafar looked nervously at his father, who nodded and gestured him to recite his vow.

"Um … I pledge, in honesty and sincerity," Jafar started, but the words stuck in his mouth. He forced himself to continue, "To be for you a faithful and helpful husband." As he finished, he looked down.

Jafar and his father returned to the other room, and the banquet was served for the men. A little bit later, the women got their meals. Jafar could not understand the reason for serving different food for men and women, but he thought he had better not ask his father. Most likely, it was something he should have known.

I'm married now, Jafar thought, trying to eat what was placed in front of him. The force that was controlling his life was getting tighter and tighter hold of him. It was squeezing him so badly that he was at risk of suffocating. He just hoped he would survive another day at the farm.

The sun had set, and Jafar sat alone on the balcony. He heard voices of happy people inside celebrating his wedding day. As soon as he had signed the contract, his father had lost all interest in him. Jafar assumed he was somewhere spending time with his clients and business partners.

"We'll leave soon. Tomorrow's a busy day," Jafar's uncle said, standing at the balcony door.

"Okay, I'll go and change my clothes," Jafar said, not too enthusiastic to return to the farm.

"We're simple farmers. Need to work hard to put food on the table," the uncle said.

Jafar would have wanted to say that his father just gave him a huge amount of money, but he knew better than to speak. He was the last person his uncle would spend that money on. Instead, he walked downstairs to the locker room where he had left his own clothes. His brother's wedding suit had made him feel respected, but now his day as a prince was over.

When Jafar took his shirt and pants from the bag, his phone dropped to the floor. His heart skipped a beat. *I can charge it here and call Dennis*, he thought, and rushed to connect the charger to the socket. Then he realized that he did not have Dennis' number. Besides, what he had said to him … the whole idea had been childish.

Disappointed, Jafar still switched on the phone to check if someone had sent him text messages. There were none.

"So, a married man, how does it feel?" Abdul said, walking into the locker room.

"Um … fine, I guess," Jafar said, handing the wedding suit to his brother. "Thanks for the loan."

"You're welcome. But you should have more muscles. It's far too big for such a tiny guy." Abdul laughed.

"Yeah, maybe I should," Jafar said.

"Don't worry. You'll get plenty of exercise working at the farm," Abdul said and laughed more.

"For sure," Jafar said bitterly.

The phone started to ring. Jafar did not recognize the sound at first, but then he picked up the phone from the floor and answered. It was Dennis.

"Um … could you please slow down? I can't understand you," Jafar said. Dennis was speaking far too fast and confusingly.

"Okay, okay, sorry…. I'm with Adler in Abyei Town, and we just killed two guys. We need your help, and we don't have much time," Dennis said.

"In Abyei Town? Are they dead?" Jafar said.

"Of course they are dead," Dennis said, confused. "Oh … we don't need your help with them, but we need to get out of here," he explained.

"Okay, what should I do?" Jafar asked.

"Contact the embassy and tell them we need help," Dennis said.

"You don't know? The embassy was attacked. It's closed. There's nobody there," Jafar said.

"Fuck. What happened?" Dennis asked. "Never mind, never mind. Can you drive here to give us a ride to Juba?"

Jafar promised get the Marines from Abyei Town even though he did not have a car. And even if he'd had one, the ride would take nearly twelve hours. There was only one road that led from Juba to Abyei, and they agreed Jafar would drive toward Abyei until he could see Dennis and Adler waiting for him. What Dennis did not mention was that there would be quite a bunch of enemy soldiers waiting for him, too.

"Take your car. We need to go to Abyei Town right now," Jafar said.

"What?" Adler said, surprised by how determined his brother suddenly sounded.

"Those American Marines that I told you about are in some kind of trouble. We need to help them."

"So? That's their problem," Abdul said coolly. "Wait. Is that guy … Dennis or something there, too?"

"Yes, he is," Jafar said tentatively. He was surprise that Abdul knew his name, but maybe he had mentioned it before.

"Okay…," Abdul said, and paused for a while. "So, he's your friend, and maybe we should help him."

"Thanks," Jafar said with a smile, thankful that Abdul changed his mind.

"Wait here. I'll get my car keys and make sure nobody sees us leaving," Abdul said.

Abdul left the locker room and checked that his car keys were still in his pocket. He went to the ballroom to find his father. They exchanged a few words, and Abdul disappeared to the kitchen. When he came back, Mr. Badri nodded to him when their eyes met. Then Abdul returned to the locker room.

"Let's go," Abdul said.

"Jafar, are you ready?" their uncle yelled from the corridor. He was approaching the locker room.

"Quick, there's a back door," Abdul said, guiding Jafar out of the building.

"Thanks," Jafar said when they were sitting in Abdul's car.

"My pleasure, brother, my pleasure," Abdul said, and started the engine.

They left Juba behind them and drove north. There was little traffic outside the capital that late in the evening, but they had to drive slowly since the gravel road was in poor shape. Abdul avoided the bumps; some of them were so big they could have easily damaged the car.

"You have a beautiful wife. You must be stoked, aren't you?" Abdul said.

"Huh? Yeah, Amira is a nice girl," Jafar said. He was so worried about Dennis that he could hardly focus on what his brother was saying.

"Have you fucked her already?" Abdul said as he yanked the steering wheel to avoid a big rock on the road.

"Not yet," Jafar said.

"Why? What's wrong? There's no celibacy in Islam."

"We just got married," Jafar said, feeling uncomfortable.

"Bro, you should become a man. Show your girl what she's been missing." Abdul laughed and poked Jafar's arm.

"Okay."

The lonely moon and the headlights of Abdul's Nissan illuminated the road. They had been driving a couple of hours, and it was midnight. Abdul stopped the car to take a leak. After a while, he returned to the car, buttoning up his pants.

"So, tell me about this Dennis," Abdul said as he started to drive.

"What about him?" Jafar said, concerned that Abdul was suddenly interested in Dennis. *Does he know about us, or am I just paranoid?*

"Does he have a family at home? Wife and kids?" Abdul asked nonchalantly.

"I guess so. I don't know him that well," Jafar lied. He was worried that Abdul could hear it in his voice.

"What about the other guy…? What was his name?" Abdul said.

"Adler," Jafar said.

"How is he?" Abdul asked.

"He's the team leader, a couple of years older," Jafar said. "He has a wife, Janet, who is pregnant," he added. Dennis had once told him about his teammates.

"Cool." Abdul kept his focus on the road.

Jafar was tired, but he could not sleep. He was too worried about what was waiting for them in Abyei Town. Dennis had not had much time to explain what had happened. They had killed two men; that much, Jafar had understood. Apparently those men had been their enemies.

"Do you wanna have children?" Abdul asked unexpectedly.

"Um … I haven't thought about it," Jafar said. Adler's personal questions started to irritate him, but he had no choice but to sit in the car with his brother.

"You should," Adler said. "Now that you have a wife and everything."

"Maybe I should."

"When a man approaches his wife, he is guarded by two angels and he is like a warrior fighting for the cause of Allah…," Abdul began.

"…and when he has intercourse with her, his sins fall like the leaves of the tree," Jafar finished for him.

Their father had taught them Islamic sexual morality over and over again ever since they were teenagers, and both Abdul and Jafar could quote a lot of what the Prophet had said. The difference was that Abdul really believed in all that while Jafar's faith had been tested a lot lately, and he was no longer so sure what to believe.

An hour later, Jafar had finally fallen asleep. Abdul looked at his brother. If what Mother had told him was true, the American had a bad influence on Jafar. That Marine was a real Devil's predator who was luring his innocent brother to the sins of sodomy. Abdul could not stand that. He had to save Jafar, if for no other reason than to protect the honor of the family.

Once I kill that son of a bitch, my brother will become a real man again, Abdul thought, and checked that he still had the knife he had taken from the kitchen.

Chapter 12

Turning the flashlight toward the door, Dennis found himself staring straight at the pipe of the machine gun the soldier was holding. There was nowhere to hide, and he saw his life flash before his eyes. Then he heard two gunshots.

"Quick, we need to hide the bodies. More guys might be coming," Adler said.

"Huh? Oh, sure," Dennis said, still holding the receiver of the phone against his ear. It took some time for him to realize that Adler had shot the guys and he was still alive.

"Put the phone away. We need to clean this mess," Adler said impatiently.

"Wait!" Dennis held up one finger, pressing the phone closer to his ear. "Jafar, is that you?"

"Yes, it's me," Jafar said softly. Dennis realized how much he had missed his voice.

"We're in Abyei Town, two soldiers are dead, Adler's injured, we need help, and you need to contact the ambassador or the Chief of—"

"Um … could you please slow down? I can't understand you," Jafar interrupted him.

Dennis explained what had happened, and Jafar promised to drive to Abyei as fast as he could so he could help the Marines with their injuries and drive them to safety. Dennis was relieved that they finally had some hope of surviving. What worried him was that Jafar would not be there before morning. The Liberation Movement soldiers might already be looking for them, and Dennis was not sure how long Adler could manage without medical support.

"The shit has hit the fan," Dennis said after he had ended the call.

"What?" Adler said.

"The embassy has been attacked. It's closed."

"Holy shit," Adler said. "The ambassador, where is he?"

"I don't know. I hope he's still alive," Dennis said.

"Okay, but let's take care of these guys now," Adler said, and pointed to the soldiers lying dead on the floor.

Dennis looked around, but the big table in the middle of the room was the only furniture. He had to pull the soldiers out of the building and find a place to hide the corpses. It was difficult in the darkness because he did not want to use the flashlight. Finally, he found a place where the bodies of the dead soldiers would be hidden at least until sunrise. Dennis hoped it would give them enough time.

"Did you see anybody?" Adler asked when Dennis returned to get him.

"No, but I heard some voices," Dennis said.

"They must've heard the gunshots, and now they're figuring out what has happened," Adler said. "We need to leave."

"Should we go back to the same place where we slept last night?" Dennis proposed.

"It's too close. We need to get as far as possible before they realize that two of their men are missing," Adler said.

"Yeah. All hell will break loose when they realize that," Dennis said.

"Exactly."

They crawled behind the building and moved toward the main road. Whenever it was possible, they stayed hidden in the long grass. Adler moved with relative agility considering he could use only his left leg to crawl. They stopped only when they were a safe distance from the building that the Liberation Movement used as their base.

"Let's check the GPS to make sure we are moving in the right direction," Adler said.

"Good idea," Dennis said as he switched on the GPS device.

"Are you able to help me get here?" Adler asked, pointing to a location on the map.

"I think so. It shouldn't be more than a mile."

Dennis was about to help Adler up when they heard the sound of incoming cars. They dropped to the ground and waited until the cars had passed them. Then they waited longer before they stood up and started to walk in the direction the cars had come from.

"Those cars were carrying more soldiers, weren't they?" Dennis said.

"Yes."

"We can't walk far enough before Jafar gets here."

"No, we can't," Adler said.

"So, do we just have to hope that they don't see Jafar driving here and picking us up?" Dennis said.

"Yep."

"Fuck. We are so doomed."

"I know."

The hope Dennis had had after talking with Jafar was rapidly fading away. Trying to find some optimism in the hopeless situation, the Marines limped forward in the darkness of Africa.

The rising sun woke up Dennis and Adler, who had been sleeping close to each other behind a Kenkiliba bush near the main road. They had walked almost two miles, after which they had been so exhausted that they had just collapsed on the grass.

Dennis helped Adler to rise, and Adler put his arms around Dennis and hugged him tightly.

"Thanks. I wouldn't have made it this far without you," Adler said, looking Dennis directly in the eyes.

Dennis kissed Adler on impulse. As soon as their lips touched, he realized it was a mistake. Adler had not pulled back, but he had not kissed him back either. He just stood there and looked confused.

"Oh, sorry," Dennis said, embarrassed. "I didn't mean to," he added and looked away.

"Um … okay," Adler said.

"Can we just forget that?"

"Yeah, I'm okay," Adler said. "I mean, I'm obviously not okay, my ankle and everything, but if I have to die here, I can for sure take one kiss." He tried to smile.

Adler was pale, and his eyes were red. He looked rather horrible, even though it was the same Adler Dennis had had a secret crush on at the Training Company. It was irony playing its wicked games that Dennis had to wait until this moment to kiss his dream boy.

"I'm taking you home," Dennis said.

"I know. You're always right," Adler said, giving a weak smile. "You will make some lucky guy a good husband someday."

"Um … thanks," Dennis said, blushing heavily.

"What? You never planned to marry some guy?"

Before Dennis had a chance to answer, they heard a car coming, and then another car from the opposite direction. Quickly, they hid behind a bush. *Dear God, don't let the other car be Jafar's*, Dennis thought, and sensed that Adler was thinking the same.

The first car, which came from the direction of the Liberation Movement base, stopped at a crossroad near the Marines. It waited there until the second car came closer, and then some soldiers emerged from the car. Dennis waited, holding his breath, as the second car approached and finally parked near the first car. Two men got out of the car.

"Neither of them is Jafar," Dennis whispered, relieved.

"No, but can you see that short, fat man who got out of the first car?"

"He seems somehow familiar," Dennis said. "Wait. Is it Shaker?"

"I think so," Adler said, pointing his Glock at the man.

"Can you kill him from this far?" Dennis asked.

"I think so. But if I shoot him, the other soldiers will realize we are here and they will kill us for sure," Adler said.

"So, we'll sacrifice our lives to accomplish the mission?" Dennis said.

"No, I can't do that." Adler put his pistol down.

Dennis did not say a word but felt relaxed. They watched as the men talked for a while and then both cars continued in the direction of the Liberation Movement base. Adler lay silently on the ground, and his face was full of pain.

"What's wrong? Has your ankle gotten worse?" Dennis asked.

"It's as bad as it can be, but that's not what's bothering me."

"What is it then?"

"I screwed up our mission," Adler said softly.

"No fucking way. You made the right choice," Dennis said.

"I'm not so sure."

"Had you shot the bastard, your child would grow up without a father," Dennis said.

Neither of them said a word; they just kept walking along the road. Every now and then, they saw abandoned houses, dead animals, shoes and clothes, and other items that proved that people had been living there not so long ago. They felt hungry as they had not eaten properly for several days, and they had run out of water, too. So, they just walked and hoped they would be saved soon.

"The road goes around that meadow. We could cut through here," Adler said.

"That's a good idea. We can still see the road," Dennis said, and they left the road.

There was a small hovel on the other edge of the meadow. Other than that, they could not see any signs of people having lived in the area. Maybe the locals had kept their cattle there for feeding. They were in the middle of the meadow when they saw a car coming. There were no good hiding places and they were so tired that Dennis just kept helping Adler walk toward the other end of the meadow.

The car stopped, and Dennis saw Jafar stepping out of the car. He was standing a couple of hundred yards from them, but Dennis was sure it was Jafar. It had to be. He waved to Jafar, and Jafar waved back. Immense joy filled his heart—they had been saved.

Dennis and Adler moved closer to the car as fast as they could with Adler's hurt ankle. They heard some distant sounds of vehicles approaching from behind them. Then a gunshot split the air, and Dennis swayed back violently. He was bleeding and, after the first rush of adrenaline, he felt heavy pain somewhere in his body.

"Fuck. What was that?" Dennis cried, crashing to the ground.

"Watch out!" Adler yelled.

A young kid, hardly thirteen, walked out of the hovel. He had a rifle in his hand, and he was loading a new pellet in it. Knowing that the boy was preparing to shoot them again, Adler raised his pistol and aimed at the boy. His hand was shaking, and he heard how the sound of the approaching trucks was getting louder and louder.

Chapter 13

Jafar watched in terror as Adler ran toward the car carrying Dennis on his back. Dennis looked limp with his arm dangling in the air. His eyes were open, and Jafar hoped more than anything that he was still alive.

"Is he dead?" Jafar cried.

"No," Adler said. "I think the bullet went through his right arm. I'm sure he's in a lot of pain, and he might be in shock."

"Oh, dear," Jafar said as he tried to pull himself together. "Let's put him in the backseat. I'll bandage it."

They saw the Liberation Movement vehicles approaching. Adler put Dennis quickly in the backseat and jumped into the front seat. He saw that someone was sitting behind the steering wheel, but he felt dizzy and his vision was getting bleary. He had run to the car carrying

Dennis, and now the pain in his ankle had reached a level that was beyond anything he could have imagined.

"Let's go…. They are…," Adler said, losing consciousness before he could finish the sentence.

Abdul turned the car and stepped on the gas. The Nissan raced toward Juba. Unfortunately, the Liberation Movement trucks kept following them. Abdul tried to drive as fast as he could on the bumpy gravel road, but the trucks following them were getting closer and closer.

While his brother tried to escape from the chasers, Jafar took off his shirt and used it to tie the wound on Dennis' arm. Abdul watched from the rearview mirror with a disapproving look on his face when Jafar shifted Dennis to his lap so he could better work with the arm.

"Thanks," Dennis said, awaking from the slumber.

"You're welcome. Good to see you alive," Jafar said softly.

"Adler, we did it," Dennis said, but Adler did not respond.

"Adler?" Dennis said. "Adler, are you okay?"

Dennis reached out toward Alder and tried to shake him, but Adler just mumbled something. Dennis checked his pulse from the neck, and it seemed to be okay.

"We can't stop, but at least he's alive," Dennis said, worried.

"Is he injured?" Jafar asked.

"His ankle is broken so he can't walk, and we haven't eaten for several days," Dennis said.

"Can't walk? He ran to the car carrying you on his back," Jafar said.

"Shit. That's not possible. His ankle was so fucking painful that he couldn't even step on it."

"He did. He must have passed out from the pain," Jafar said.

They heard gunshots from behind. Some bullets hit the car, and Dennis pulled Jafar's head down. In other circumstances, Dennis might have found lying on top of each other in the backseat of the car rather romantic. Now it was mostly scary because he was starting to realize they could not escape the chasers.

"Can we go any faster?" Dennis asked when the next series of bullets broke the rear window.

"You really think I'm not driving as fast as this car goes?" Abdul said, irritated.

They were now several miles south of Abyei Town, and the hills were getting higher. There were even some mountains on the horizon. The road followed the valley between the hills, and it was full of deep curves, which gave them some cover. It would not help them for long, though, as the first truck was only two hundred yards from them.

"We are trapped. There are more soldiers coming in front of us," Abdul said when they came to a clearing.

"There are dozens of cars. What do we do now?" Jafar cried.

"Wait. Those are Ethiopians," Dennis said. "Turn left and stop the car there."

"Stop?" Abdul said, amazed. "The guys behind us will kill us."

"I think the Ethiopians are looking for them. When Salih's men see the Ethiopians, they'll have no choice but to turn back," Dennis said.

Dennis was right. The Liberation Movement lost their interest in hunting them as soon as they realized that a battalion of African Union forces was waiting for them. They waited until the Ethiopians had passed by, and then they continued their journey to Juba.

They had hardly driven a mile when Abdul started to talk to Jafar. He was speaking Arabic, and Dennis could not understand what they were saying. Even so, he was aware of the agitated tone of the discussion. It did not take long before Abdul started to shout at Jafar.

"Watch out! He has a knife, and he is going to kill us!" Jafar cried in English.

"Give me the knife and keep driving," Adler said, pointing his gun at Abdul. The argument between the brothers had wakened him, but he still felt weak.

"Those guys are sodomites. They deserve to die," Abdul said angrily, looking for support from Adler.

"If you want to live, don't talk like that about my friend," Adler said. "And now, give me the knife."

"Bloody Americans, spreading your filthy lifestyle. God will punish you one day," Abdul muttered, gave the knife to Adler, and kept driving.

The fact that his brother knew he was gay made Jafar shake from fear. Abdul had said that the family had suspected it for years. *I have nowhere to go, and I'm not safe anywhere. My life's over*, Jafar thought, and felt how Dennis put his arm around him.

It was already midnight when they arrived in Juba. Abdul left them in front of what was left of the embassy and told Jafar something that made him anxious. Then he drove away, leaving the three of them to bemoan the destruction. The Marines could not understand how someone had managed to destroy the entire main building. It must have required several explosives detonated at the same time in strategic positions.

"Fuck. They have blown up the whole damn thing," Dennis said, not believing his eyes. "Was the ambassador there when it happened?"

"Huh? Yes, I think he was," Jafar said, distracted.

"And the Chief of Staff, too?" Dennis said.

"Yes," Jafar said, looking around nervously.

"Your brother said something intimidating before he left," Adler said to Jafar. "He threatened to kill you?"

"He and my father," Jafar said, "and by morning, all my relatives and neighbors will join them."

"I'm so sorry that I dragged you into this. I should've thought," Dennis said, embarrassed.

They stood in front of the main gate, and nobody knew what to say next. They just stared at each other, Adler feeling sorry for Jafar and Dennis feeling embarrassed that he had, once again, let his penis lead the way. But he had not just been hunting for sex. There was something different in Jafar, something that appealed to him and he could not resist.

"Let's try to find a phone at the medical center. We need to call for help," Adler said.

"Um … I have a cellphone," Jafar said, offering his phone to Adler. He felt embarrassed that he had not thought of it before.

"Great," Adler said. "Dennis, help me into the building. I need some medicine and something to drink."

Jafar found painkillers from the medicine cabinet and brought the drugs and water to Adler, who sat on a couch in the lounge. Dennis used a chair to break the glass of the vending machine and brought them soda pops and snacks. Jafar went to search for a clean bandage for Dennis' arm while the Marines ate everything they could find.

"You remember that child who shot at you in Abyei?" Adler said. "I … what I did…."

"You did not have a choice," Dennis said, removing the wrapper from his fourth chocolate bar.

"But it was just a child," Adler said.

"I know," Dennis said. He could not argue about that.

"If someone did that to my child, I don't know what I would do."

"That kid was an enemy. He was a soldier," Dennis tried to console him.

"You really think that the child had decided to become a killer?" Adler asked, staring at Dennis.

"Sorry, I wasn't thinking. Of course not."

Jafar came back and changed the bandage on Dennis' arm. Adler could not help smiling when he noticed how gently Jafar took care of Dennis. He recognized that the tenderness between the two men was similar to what his wife showed him when he was sick or tired.

"I'll call us help," Adler said as he entered the Marine Corps emergency number in Jafar's cellphone.

"Emergency service, how can I help you?" the operator answered the call.

"This is Sergeant Williams, and I'm calling from South Sudan. We need medical help and evacuation to Camp Pendleton as soon as possible."

"Sir, please tell me your current position and the name of the operation."

"We are at the US Embassy in Juba, and the name of the operation is Silent Moon," Adler said.

"Just a minute please," the operator said.

The line went silent. Most likely is was not more than two minutes, but for Adler it felt like he had waited at least fifteen minutes before the operator finally returned on the line.

"I'm sorry, sir, but we don't have operations in South Sudan. Can you tell me your name and ID number please?"

"Sergeant Adler Williams, ID 7752167," Adler said.

"I'm sorry sir, but your ID is not in the system," the operator said after a while. "Is this some joke? Where did you get this number?"

Adler ended the call and looked at Dennis in amazement.

"Our mission is not in the system," he said, "and apparently we are no longer in the system either."

"What do we do now?" Dennis asked.

"I'll call the Battalion Commander at Camp Pendleton," Adler said.

It was a sunny afternoon in California when Lieutenant Colonel Malcolm Davies answered the call in his office. He was surprised to hear Adler's voice on the line. Marine Corps Special Operations Command had reported Sergeant Williams dead just a couple of days ago, and he had delivered the message to Adler's wife and parents.

"Williams, I thought you died when the Embassy was attacked. That's what they told me," Colonel Davies said.

"Negative, sir, our Yankee was shot down near Abyei. Newton and Mullen died in the accident. Corporal Benson and I survived," Adler explained.

"What the hell were you doing in Abyei?" Colonel Davies said.

"Sir, can we talk about that later. We need urgent medical help and transport," Adler said politely.

"Okay, just wait a moment. I'll find someone who can arrange that for you," Colonel Davies said.

Soon they had instructions to arrive at Juba airport where a military plane had a scheduled departure to the US in a couple of hours. Colonel Davies had arranged medics on the plane. Adler's ankle would require a bigger operation, but that was hardly possible until they arrived at Camp Pendleton.

"Let's go. They sent us a car to take us to the airport," Adler said, and waited for Dennis to help him stand up.

Jafar stood at the front door of the medical center and looked at the Marines who walked slowly toward the black SUV that had parked where the main gate had been. They did not even turn to say goodbye to him, even though he had just saved their lives. *I need to save myself next. I'll be dead if my father finds me*, he thought.

Chapter 14

The driver opened the front door, and Dennis helped Adler
sit down. He was about to climb into the back of the car
when he noticed that Jafar was still standing at the door of
the medical center.

"You don't want to come with us?" he shouted to Jafar.
His voice was full of disappointment.

"To America?" Jafar asked, hardly believing what he
had just been offered.

Dennis nodded. Before the Marines knew it, Jafar was
sitting in the backseat next to Dennis.

It took them half an hour to get to the airport. Adler had
to explain to the pilot several times how Jafar had saved
their lives and that he was in danger because his family
was trying to kill him. Finally, the pilot agreed to take him
with them, but told them that Jafar might be refused entry

to the US when they arrived at Camp Pendleton's military airport.

Dennis helped Adler climb the stairs to the Gulfstream C-37A transport aircraft, and the pilot started the Rolls-Royce turbofan engines. Even though it was an ultra-long range jet, configured for 16 passengers, they still had to fly via London and Miami to refuel the tanks. It did not matter to any of them. They were safe now.

Jafar watched from the window how Juba got smaller and smaller before it disappeared behind the clouds. He had just left his old life behind him, and he had no idea what was waiting for him.

"You like him, don't you?" Adler said when he noticed how Dennis was staring at Jafar.

"He's a nice guy," Dennis said, and blushed.

"And he obviously likes you," Adler said.

"Are you some Cupid now? Pairing me up with him?"

"If I have to," Adler said. "Why don't you go and sit with him?"

Dennis hesitated a bit but finally stood up and took a seat next to Jafar. He did not want to look back, but he was sure that Adler was following his actions. Actually, he felt like all the other passengers were watching him, too, which made him very self-conscious. Jafar smiled at him shyly.

"Hi, um … how are you?" Dennis said.

"My first time on an airplane," Jafar said.

"Scared?"

"My brother and father will soon be thousands of miles away. I have no reason to be scared," Jafar said. "Besides, you're sitting there."

"I'll keep you safe," Dennis said with a smile.

"I know," Jafar said, and touched Dennis' hand.

Jafar's touch was electric, and Dennis felt how Jafar moved his leg closer to his. Dennis was getting slightly aroused, and it did not help that images of making out with Jafar at the embassy filled his mind. The cute boy was looking at him curiously with his big eyes.

"I never stopped thinking of you, even when I married Amira, which I did because my family forced me to marry her," Jafar said, like he owed Dennis an explanation.

"It sucks that they made you to do that," Dennis said, avoiding talking about his feelings.

"She's a sweet girl, but the marriage and living at my uncle's farm made me miserable."

"I can hardly believe what you have gone through," Dennis said.

Jafar's eyes lingered on the sexy Marine who was smiling at him. His whole life everybody around him, especially his father, had taught him how homosexuality is dirty and sinful. He had done his best to deny his feelings for Dennis, but he could not do it anymore. Besides, there was no need for it anymore. For the first time in his life, he felt completely free.

Both of them were tired as they had not been sleeping since escaping from the Liberation Movement soldiers. Soon, they fell asleep in their seats, leaning against each other. They did not even wake when the flight attendant brought a blanket and laid it on them.

"Gentlemen, we will land in London in fifty minutes. Would you like to have some coffee or tea?" the flight attendant said sometime later, gently poking Dennis on his shoulder.

Dennis woke up and flinched when he saw the attendant dressed in the US Air Force uniform. His look was sharp but friendly. Dennis was embarrassed that the man had found them sleeping against each other.

"Um … we would like to have some tea please," Dennis said, realizing that it made them sound like a couple.

"Here you are, gentlemen," the flight attendant said, putting two cups of tea on the table in front of Dennis. "I'll bring your breakfast shortly," he added.

The flight attendant walked to the front of the plane where there was a small kitchen. Dennis scanned his butt and muscular body. The guy looked hot in the uniform. Dennis blushed slightly when he realized that the man had noticed him staring. Apparently, he did not mind, and he soon returned with two trays.

"And here is your breakfast, gentlemen. Bon appétit," the flight attendant said, smiling.

"Thank you," Dennis said and checked the man again when he left to serve other passengers.

"He's cute, isn't he?" Jafar said and grinned at Dennis. Dennis blushed, which made Jafar's grin even wider.

"I think you are cuter," Dennis said and blushed even more.

Jafar was pleased to hear that and even more pleased when Dennis next leaned closer and kissed him. It was a short kiss, but it meant a lot to both of them.

They refueled the aircraft at the Royal Air Force Northolt station in South Ruislip, six miles north of London Heathrow airport. After departure, Jafar fell asleep again, and Dennis watched him for a while before he went to sit next to Adler.

"Look. We should talk about something," Dennis said tentatively.

"Okay," Adler said.

"About the kiss," Dennis said, and looked embarrassed.

"You mean the kiss you gave Jafar before we landed?" Adler teased, even though he knew what Dennis meant.

"I mean kissing you."

"Don't worry. I totally understand. You took advantage of an injured guy who couldn't escape and who happened to be extremely handsome," Adler said with a grin.

"Smartass," Dennis said. Adler gave him a friendly smile.

Apparently, his attempt to come on to Adler had not bothered the sergeant. He was relieved. He had been worried that the mistake he had made on impulse would break their friendship.

"And we don't have to tell my wife or your boyfriend," Adler said, smiling.

"He's not my boyfriend," Dennis protested.

"Yet," Adler said, and poked Dennis on his arm. "And now you could help me to the bathroom," he added.

"Only if you stop talking shit," Dennis said, getting up.

"Think about it. You're a good guy, Corporal Benson. You deserve to be happy," Adler said as he let Dennis help him to the bathroom. Dennis had to admit that Adler was making a good point. He had feelings for Jafar.

Lieutenant Colonel Davies was waiting for them when they landed at the military airport at Camp Pendleton in California. As the Commanding Officer for the First Reconnaissance Battalion, Colonel Davies was their field officer. He greeted the Marines and Jafar shortly and took them to the office of Major General Daniels, who was the Commander of the First Marine Division.

"Good afternoon, sir. Here they come," Colonel Davies said.

"Please sit down and just give me a minute," General Daniels said, hardly lifting his eyes from the paper he was reading.

"He's the commander of the division to which our battalion belongs," Dennis whispered to Jafar after they had taken their seats on a big sofa.

"I got a report saying that MARSOC sent you on a mission just before the embassy was attacked," General Daniels said, going directly into the business.

"That is correct, sir," Adler said.

"What happened to Privates Newton and Mullen?" General Daniels said.

"The helicopter that transported us was shot down. They died in the crash," Adler said.

"And who is that guy?" General Daniels said, pointing at Jafar but addressing the question to Adler.

"He's Jafar Badri, sir," Adler said. "He's an embassy worker who saved our lives after the helicopter crashed."

General Daniels studied Jafar but did not say anything. He took the paper that he had been reading and checked something before he continued.

"Does he speak English?" General Daniels said.

"Um … yes, I do … sir," Jafar said.

"Then tell me, son: why are you here?"

"I want to apply for asylum, sir," Jafar said. "My life is in danger."

"Why do you think so?" General Daniels said, surprised.

"I'm gay," Jafar said.

General Daniels looked at Colonel Davies as if asking whether he knew this turn of events was coming. Colonel Davies raised his hands. Jafar was so nervous that he had difficulty finding a comfortable position on the sofa.

There was a knock on the door, and General Daniels' secretary looked in. She said the medical team had arrived and they would take Dennis and Adler to the hospital where they could tend to Dennis' gunshot wound and Adler's broken ankle. In addition to the necessary surgeries, both of them had lived several days without clean water and food.

"Where did you plan to live?" General Daniels asked Jafar, ignoring the secretary.

"Sir, he'll live with me," Dennis said, and everybody turned to look at him.

Dennis saw a grin on Adler's face, and Jafar smiled at him. Dennis had no choice but to smile back, ignoring General Daniels and Colonel Davies, who were looking at him.

Chapter 15

It was a cloudy Friday morning, almost two weeks after they had arrived in California. Dennis' arm was healing from the surgery, and it was his last day of sick leave. He and Jafar were spending it in Dennis' bedroom, which had now become their bedroom.

Dennis found it funny how amazed Jafar had been about everything: the house, his car, the big TV in the living room, and even the food Dennis had brought from the grocery store. Gradually, he had gotten used to his new life in the US.

"It's so true what they say ... black guys are well-equipped," Dennis said and kissed Jafar.

"You keep saying that," Jafar murmured softly.

"I could lie naked in this bed with you the whole day," Dennis said, and took Jafar's penis in his hand. It started to grow.

"I bet you could," Jafar said as he pushed Dennis' hand away. "I need some breakfast. I'm starving."

"I know what made you hungry," Dennis said with a grin.

Jafar smiled and felt how his erection kept growing. He felt happy and safe. He loved lying in bed with the sexy Marine even though at first he had been a bit unsure. He had never had sex before, but Dennis had been very gentle and extra careful not to push Jafar to do anything that made him uncomfortable. It had not taken long for him to get used to it. Dennis' hands wandering around his body had felt far too good.

Dennis stood up and opened the curtains to let the light in. Unfortunately, it also revealed that nobody had cleaned there for weeks. A layer of dust covered the wooden floor and other surfaces.

"Yeah, it's about time to clean our house," Dennis said, noticing that Jafar was looking at the condition of the room as well.

"Speaking of *our* house…," Jafar said tentatively. "We have not talked about how long I can live here."

"As long as you want," Dennis said, avoiding the real question that Jafar had in his mind.

"How long do you want me to?" Jafar asked.

Dennis sat down on the bed and put his arm around Jafar. His face went severe as he was not used to talking about his feelings. He was thinking about how to answer Jafar's question.

"I need to confess something," Dennis said. "I have never dated anyone."

"Me, neither," Jafar said. "Well, except I've been married a couple of hours," he corrected.

"Technically speaking, you are still married," Dennis said.

"I'm not so sure," Jafar said. He assumed that his father and uncle had already taken care of that.

"Anyway, that was not my point. I'm … I guess I'm trying to say that I would like to try dating with you," Dennis said.

"Oh," Jafar said.

"I mean, if that's okay with you," Dennis said, afraid that Jafar would not like the idea.

"It's more than okay," Jafar said, and smiled widely. "It's much more than I'd dared dream of."

They looked at each other, both of them with dopey smiles on their faces. Soon Dennis pushed Jafar back on the bed. Unfortunately, the doorbell interrupted their make-out session. Dennis dressed in his robe and went to answer the door. Jafar put his new jeans on and followed him shortly.

"Morning, sir, how are you?" Dennis said, surprised to find Colonel Davies standing at the door.

"Good morning, Dennis," Colonel Davies said. "Oh … morning, Jafar," he added when he saw Jafar standing shirtless in the living room.

"Um … we were just planning to have some breakfast," Dennis said, and blushed slightly.

"Correct me if I'm wrong, but Jafar will not live here just temporarily," Colonel Davies said to Dennis.

"Huh? Oh, umm … no. I hope that's not a problem." Dennis' blush deepened.

"Don't ask, don't tell is over," Colonel Davies said with an approving smile on his face.

Dennis invited the colonel in, and they sat at the kitchen table. He offered coffee to the colonel, who accepted even though he had apparently drank too much already. Colonel Davies took some papers from his briefcase and spread them out on the table.

"I talked with an immigration attorney yesterday. She'll help you with the application, and she said you shouldn't have a problem getting refugee status," Colonel Davies said to Jafar.

"Thank you, sir. That sounds great," Jafar said, delighted.

"Jafar, thank you. I'm grateful that you brought two of my men home alive," Colonel Davies said.

"Me too," Dennis said.

"Actually, I would like to offer you a job, if you're interested. The hospital at Camp Pendleton needs more nurses," Colonel Davies said.

"Of course I'm interested. Thank you so much, sir," Jafar said.

"Let's talk about it more once your asylum application is processed and you get the necessary papers," Colonel Davies said.

Jafar thanked the colonel again, and then he left for a shower. He had a hard time concealing his happiness. He was in America, Dennis had just asked him to be his boyfriend, and soon he would even have a job. His life had changed so rapidly that he could not even believe that it was true. *If I'm dreaming, never wake me up*, he thought as he felt the warm water on his body.

"Have we learned who attacked the embassy in Juba?" Dennis asked when he was alone with the colonel.

"Unfortunately not, or at least I've not been told," Colonel Davies said, looking a bit uncomfortable.

"That's too bad. They made quite a disaster," Dennis said.

"The good thing, if there is such, is that, because of the strike to the embassy, the UN and the African Union authorized stronger military actions to stop the conflict in South Sudan."

"So they started to mess with the wrong guys," Dennis observed.

"We can't just watch from the sidelines when somebody blows up our embassy," Colonel Davies said.

They finished their coffees, and then Colonel Davies had to return to his office. Dennis wanted to ask if the colonel really was okay with his living together with Jafar, but he could not find the right words. Besides, the colonel had already answered that question.

"Oh, just one more thing," Colonel Davies said. "General Christensen from Special Operations asked me to see if you accomplished the goal of your mission. Whatever that was."

"Unfortunately not. Please tell him we never found the target," Dennis said.

"Okay, I'll let him know," Colonel Davies said and left.

Jafar had just finished the shower as the front door closed, and he walked to the living room with his towel wrapped around his waist. Dennis stared at his half-naked body with pure lust in his eyes. Jafar noticed his gaze and dropped the towel on the floor. That was all that was needed for Dennis to push him back to the bedroom.

The following morning, Dennis waited in the lobby of the Camp Pendleton military hospital and watched as the doctors and nurses hurried from one patient room to another. The phones at the reception desk were ringing, and the air was filled with announcements paging staff members and asking visitors to take care of their personal belongings.

Dennis had waited almost half an hour before Adler was finally wheeled to the lobby, holding crutches on his lap. He looked much better than a week ago, and he smiled when he saw Dennis.

"How's your ankle?" Dennis asked.

"Better," Adler said and signed the paper the nurse gave him. "They operated on it a couple of times, and they expect a full recovery."

"Nice," Dennis said. "When will you be back?"

"Um … I don't know," Adler said, looking uncomfortable.

"You're planning to quit?" Dennis said. His face was severe.

"I am," Adler said.

Adler stood up and, using the crutches, walked with Dennis to the park behind the hospital where they sat down on a bench. Dennis understood now why Adler had asked him to pick him up from the hospital; Adler had wanted to tell him this. What Adler had just said made Dennis sad, even though he had a fair idea why Adler was thinking of leaving the Marines. Neither of them said anything for a long time.

"It's because of the kid that you…," Dennis said but could not finish the sentence.

"The kid I killed." Adler looked down. "That's one reason."

"He would have shot us if you hadn't," Dennis said.

"I know, but that kid was barely twelve. And I made a decision to end his life."

"Don't be too hard on yourself."

"How couldn't I? I killed one child, and I might've made another an orphan," Adler said.

"You mean the girl and the old lady?" Dennis said.

Adler nodded. "Dennis, I can't help thinking if those kids had been mine…."

Adler would become a father in the summer when Janet gave birth to their first child. Dennis remembered how Adler had confessed just before the trip to Juba that he wished Janet had had an abortion. It seemed he had changed his mind.

"How's it going with Jafar?" Adler asked to change the topic to something lighter.

"Huh? Good," Dennis said, and blushed.

"So, you're an item?"

"I really like him."

"Wow. Corporal Benson is talking about his feelings," Adler said with a grin.

"Dumbass," Dennis said, punching Adler on his arm.

"How about your parents? Have you told them about Jafar?"

"Hell no. They'll never accept me living with another guy," Dennis said. "But I don't give a shit."

Adler's phone started to ring. It was Janet, asking if he had told Dennis already. He explained that he had just been released and they were talking about it right then. She told him that lunch would be ready soon and asked him to hurry.

"The ceremony for Newton and Mullen is next week," Adler said as they were walking to the parking area.

"We lost two great guys," Dennis said sadly.

"We did," Adler agreed.

"And now if you are leaving, the entire team is gone."

"But we will still be friends," Adler said.

"Yeah, always."

What they had experienced together during the days and nights in Abyei Town was something that neither of them could easily forget. The fact that none of the great guys would be his teammates any longer felt melancholic, but Dennis was delighted that he finally had a friend with whom he could be himself. With Adler, he did not have to hide that Jafar was part of his life. It felt great.

It was Sunday evening, and Dennis would have to return to work on the following morning. He was holding Jafar on his lap, and they were watching television. His right hand was inside Jafar's pants, and he had been slowly rubbing Jafar's erection for almost an hour.

"Um … I can't take that much longer," Jafar said. His boxers were wet from precum.

"Oh, is my boyfriend horny again?" Dennis said, loving how Jafar's penis throbbed in his hand.

"Maybe," Jafar said, trying to change his position. Dennis' phone started to ring in the kitchen.

"Wait here, horny boy," Dennis said as he rose reluctantly from the sofa.

The phone kept ringing on the table near the fridge where Dennis had left it. He picked the phone up and looked at the screen. The call was from his father. He hesitated for several seconds, considering letting it go to voicemail before he finally decided to answer the call.

"Hi, Dennis, how're you?" his father said.

"I'm okay. What do you want?" he blurted out.

He had not meant to start a fight, but as soon as he heard his father's voice, all the bitterness he had felt for his parents rushed to his mind. He heard how his father sighed on the other end of the line, and he forced himself to calm down.

"I would like to talk with you, Dennis, if that's okay with you," Mr. Benson said.

"I guess it's okay," Dennis said, not trying to hide the annoyance in his voice.

"Some weeks ago, I got a message from the Marine Corps that you had died," his father said.

"Apparently, I didn't."

"Apparently not. Well, some Sergeant Williams called me this morning and told me that, too," Mr. Benson said.

Colonel Davies had told Dennis about the message he had delivered to his parents. Dennis had promised to call his parents and let them know that it was a mistake and that he was alive, but he hadn't. It seemed that Adler had done it on his behalf, which confused Dennis. He could not understand why Adler had done it.

"I thought you and Mom would not be interested," Dennis said bitterly.

"Dennis, I can't blame you for feeling that way. And I'm sorry about it," Mr. Benson said.

"Okay."

"I know this might be a lot to ask, but I was hoping that your mother and I could come to visit you someday," Mr. Benson said.

"I'm still gay, and I'm living with my boyfriend," Dennis said. "Are you okay with that?"

Dennis assumed that his father would cancel the visit, but he was tired of hiding who he was. Jafar was too important to him and his parents had better accept them both, or Dennis wanted to have nothing to do with them. What his father said next surprised him.

"I heard about that, and I guess I don't have a choice," Mr. Benson said with a nervous laugh.

"No, you don't," Dennis said, feeling a bit of hope. "Can I ask what changed your mind?"

"I thought that I had lost you, and I don't want that to happen again. Besides, Sergeant Williams said some very nice things about you."

Adler had told Mr. Benson how Dennis had saved his life after their helicopter had crashed. Without Dennis, his unborn child would have never seen her father. The way Williams had unconditionally supported Dennis had made a big impact on Mr. Benson. He understood that there were people who were obviously straight and still trusted their lives in the hands of his son.

"It would be nice if you and Mom could come visit us," Dennis said, and thanked Adler in his mind.

"Thanks, Dennis. That means a lot to your mom … and me, too," Mr. Benson said.

"And me," Dennis said.

They ended the call, and Dennis returned to the living room where he found Jafar still watching the television. He sat on the sofa and hugged Jafar. Operation Silent Moon had failed, but as far as Dennis was concerned, it could not have ended better.

About the Author

Jay Argent is a novelist in his thirties who lives a peaceful life with his husband. His favorite hobbies are music, movies, and romantic novels. He obtained a degree in engineering in 2001 and built a successful career in a management consulting firm. Using his own high school and college experiences as inspiration, he is now pursuing his true passion of writing.

If you have any feedback, you can contact him by email at jay.argent@outlook.com. He very much looks forward to hearing from you.

http://jayargent.com

Made in the USA
Middletown, DE
18 November 2023

43022364R00117